"You trying ~~to~~ an unsteady voice.

Gillian smiled, slow and a little unsteady herself. "Is it working?"

Gently he lowered her to the ground, and his mouth took hers. It was a long and hungry kiss that involved grinding tongues and grinding hips, and when his hands touched her breasts, they weren't so gentle, weren't so tender. This was pain, the most beautiful sort of pain. *Desire.* She caught her lip between her teeth, silencing her cries, silencing her moans.

Gillian had waited years for this, dreamed of it, imagined it a hundred different ways—being with Austen. But this surpassed any image, any idea she'd ever had. He was here. With her. He was finally here...and would he stay? Would she want him to?

Blaze

Dear Reader,

Bon Jovi has a very cool song, "Who Says You Can't Go Home?" As I wrote this story, the melody and lyrics kept playing in my head. Austen Hart ran away to his namesake (sort of) town, Austin, Texas, trying to erase his heritage, but no matter how fast he ran, it still haunted him. The image of who we are as we grow up is a powerful thing, not easily forgotten, and it wasn't until Austen found love that he made peace with who he was—partly thanks to our heroine, local girl Gillian Wanamaker.

Writing about Texas is always fun for me. I get to use *y'all* and *fixing to* and all those great phrases that I grew up with when I was just a young whippersnapper. Whenever I get on the phone and use the word *y'all* people stop, and then I explain and it always cracks me up, because there are no good substitutes for *y'all*.

Anyway, I hope you enjoy the second book in the Harts of Texas miniseries. In September, y'all come back for Brooke's story. You hear?

Enjoy!

Kathleen O'Reilly

Kathleen O'Reilly

JUST LET GO...

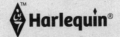

TORONTO NEW YORK LONDON
AMSTERDAM PARIS SYDNEY HAMBURG
STOCKHOLM ATHENS TOKYO MILAN MADRID
PRAGUE WARSAW BUDAPEST AUCKLAND

Recycling programs
for this product may
not exist in your area.

ISBN-13: 978-0-373-79629-8

JUST LET GO...

This edition published by arrangement with Harlequin Books S.A.

For questions and comments about the quality of this book
please contact us at Customer_eCare@Harlequin.ca.

www.Harlequin.com

Printed in U.S.A.

ABOUT THE AUTHOR

Kathleen O'Reilly wrote her first romance at the age of eleven, which to her undying embarrassment was read aloud to her class. After taking more than twenty years to recover from the profound distress, she is now proud to finally announce her career—romance author. Now she is an award-winning author of nearly twenty romances published in countries all over the world. Kathleen lives in New York with her husband and their two children, who outwit her daily.

Books by Kathleen O'Reilly

To Texans everywhere, near and far, because
when you're a Texan, you can always come home.

Prologue

SHE'D BOUGHT THE DRESS six months ago. The perfect halter-tied prom dress in candlelight blue and silver. It had taken her four shopping trips to Midland to find it, but when she saw it, she knew. When she walked, the flounce billowed like a cloud. The sleek bodice accentuated her chest before sliding smooth as silk over her hips. There it clung just enough to show the entire senior class just what hours of exercise could do. Lovingly her fingers had glided over the material, imagining his face when he saw her. She loved the hungry way he looked at her sometimes, as if she was more than a mere mortal, as if she was a queen.

By the ripe old age of seventeen, Gillian was accustomed to men taking a second glance, or whistling when she wore the extra short shorts, which she did on occasion because she liked the whistling, even though her Momma said it wasn't exactly proper behavior. In West Texas, the girls weren't supposed to be fast, like in Houston or Dallas, but boredom and hot nights were a fertile combination, and sometimes nature ruled. Nonetheless,

Gillian had a strict code of conduct, which she'd never been tempted to break...

...until now.

The sun was long gone, the moon high in a starless night. During the summer, when the dust kicked up beyond the heavens, the whole Texas sky glowed pink. Like a dream. It was nights like this that Gillian felt she was living her dreams.

He emerged from the horizon, his shoulders slumped low, until he saw her. Gillian leaned back on her elbows, breasts to the sky, posing like the pictorials in *Playboy*, even though she'd never admit to studying the sultry photos.

When he saw her, she noticed his effort to act cool, but he picked up the pace. Anxious, she could tell. As he strode toward her, her heart skipped a beat, because there was no boy that was better looking, no boy that kicked up her pulse, no boy that made her ache between her thighs like he did—not even Jeffrey Campbell Maxwell III, who was the star quarterback of the Lions. Everybody expected Gillian to go to the senior prom with Jeff Junior—except for Gillian. Gillian's heart was set in a different direction. His.

He was long and rangy, not as bulked up as some of the jocks, but there was something different about him. His muscles were crafted from hard work instead of blocking linebackers. His hands were rough from metal rather than free weights.

"What took you so long?" she asked, wondering if he noticed that she wasn't wearing a bra under her shirt. In her mind, there might as well have been a big neon arrow pointing at her tight nipples.

When he looked at her, his eyes landed somewhere

between her shoulders and her belly, and she noticed the quick, nervous bob in his throat.

Good.

"Got held up at the garage," he said.

Gillian smiled and held out a hand in invitation. "I'm glad you're here."

He sat down on the ground next to her, long legs outstretched in front of him. His once-white T-shirt was stained with dirt and grease from the shop, but there were men who were sexy even in grime, and apparently, he was one. And at least for tonight, he was hers.

She shot him one hot look from beneath her lashes, and he wiped his palms on his jeans, once, twice, and then his mouth was on hers, devouring, and demanding a response. He never kissed her like the others, not like Jeff Junior, not like Roger, not like Sonny. Gillian had never truly appreciated the art of kissing until the first time she'd touched his lips with her own.

It had been fire.

After she finally caught her breath, his hot mouth tracked her slim neck, following the line of her collarbone, down to where the pulse was drumming at her throat. She wound their hands together, her rose-tipped nails in sharp contrast to the dirt beneath his. But she didn't mind. She loved the way his big hands touched her, hesitantly, reverently like she were his altar. God would probably strike her dead for comparing the carnal arts—or nearly carnal arts, she corrected—to a place of holy worship, but Gillian knew her biology and if God didn't want teenagers running amok, he wouldn't have juiced them with roller-coaster hormones, like hers.

Not willing to wait any longer, she pulled him on top of her, feeling the rangy strength, the tensile bunching of muscles that seemed poised like a cougar ready to spring. Gillian knew she was playing fast and loose, but tonight the iron-clad Gillian Wanamaker will was noticeably absent. For once, she wanted to nibble at the apple, but not just with any man. Only him.

"I've made up my mind," she whispered in his ear, feathering kisses along the jaw.

"About what?" he whispered back, his hand sliding slyly down her blouse, touching her with that same nervous intensity. "About this?" he asked, his fingers tip-toeing across her nipples, touching them, then falling away. She drew in a breath at the exquisite sensations, the burst of heat, the feeling that she was about to explode.

"You shouldn't do that," she protested without a lick of sincerity, pushing her breasts farther into his hand, marveling at the fit. Gillian worked very hard at most things, being good included, but when she was near him, it was like summer lightning. Surprising, beautiful and dangerous. Gillian loved herself some summer lightning.

He smiled at her then, surprising, beautiful, dangerous. Then his hands worked the buttons on her shirt with both speed and dexterity that proved he was a boy who knew his way around a bra. She liked that about him, that confidence he kept stored away.

At school, his shoulders were always down, his eyes somewhere beyond the horizon. She knew he was whip-smart, but he'd never asked to be called on in class, he never opted to read aloud. In gym, he was fast, his movements quicker than most, but wasn't on any team. In fact, most people didn't give him the time of day— except for "those girls." Those girls gave him everything he wanted...or so everyone said.

Tramps, that was her momma's description, and

before you could say, "Gillian is a tramp," her blouse
was open and he was staring at her bare chest with
lusty-eyed awe. In the face of such absolute adoration, it
was hard to be shameful. Besides, Gillian believed that
adoration was meant to be graciously acknowledged,
not ignored. The moon winked down on them, the buf-
falo grass tickling the backs of her bare knees, and she
watched the sharp lines of hunger in his face. He wasn't
a boy who openly showed need, and she loved that it
was her who made him want.

Carefully his hands traced the circles of her nipples,
the outlines where rosy pink met baby's-butt white. At
first, she assumed this was part of the adoration ritual,
but soon she realized the delicious truth of the matter.
These little touches were invading her from the outside
in, zipping through her skin, her nerves. In their wake,
a wave of pressure was building in her belly, growing
stronger, dropping lower until she could feel the tight
heartbeat between her thighs.

"Take me to the prom." She spoke urgently, not the
sophisticated invitation that she'd rehearsed in her mind.
But right this second, her mind was preoccupied with
those tight little circles he was drawing on her, the way
he caught his lip between his teeth in what had to be a
painful manner.

As if sensing her difficulties, his fingers stilled
over her breast, resting there possessively. "Hell, no.
Nobody's ever going to see me in some stupid prom
duds. Not even for you, Gilly."

The words kick-started her brain. Rejection is what
some might call it. Others, notably of Gillian's persuasion, considered such talk a challenge, and one to be
welcomed—before being clobbered, of course. Pride
and prudence battled it out in her head, but prudence

never stood a chance. "Go with me," she urged, putting her hand over his, inviting him to prom, inviting him to more.

There was a moment when his fingers tightened on her own aching skin, when his eyes darkened with the secrets she wanted to know, but then everything stopped.

"No way, Gillian. Let's drive to Austin. Find a hotel. Stay all weekend. Maybe longer. Maybe forever." He looked away as he spoke, his face turned to the line of mesquite trees, not appreciating anything, the lurid nakedness of her breasts, the genius of her plans, and if Gillian hadn't put so much time and effort into both, she probably would have been a little more reasonable.

"Austin? I don't know anybody there. I want to be here. Home. At my senior prom. It'll be fun watching all the faces when we walk in."

He pulled away, leaving her alone on the ground. "I can tell you about the faces." His voice was almost angry. "The boys will be drooling, their dicks in their eyes. The girls will pretend they don't care, but they do." Still not looking at her, he plucked a blade of grass, and put it to his lips and blew. The breathy whistle cut through the silence, as if he didn't care what anyone thought, but Gillian knew better. Everybody cared, some just buried it deeper than others.

"You think the girls won't be jealous of me?" she asked, in her best girlfriend's voice. "You don't ever notice the crowd that gathers at Dot's when you're working at the shop with your shirt off?"

A dark flush rose on his cheeks. "Maybe."

Pleased with his reaction, she drew closer, until the strong tendons of his arm were hard against her breast, until the warmth of his body filled her with electricity, like she was touching the live wire and feeling the shock. She liked that touch. She needed that touch. "Come with me."

He sat motionless, unmoved by her plea, and silently she swore. There was a very precise list of things that Gillian wanted with a white-hot passion: a summer job at the bank, class salutatorian, the gold tiara at the senior prom and this boy.

So what price was she willing to pay? It was an age-old question that women had battled since the dawn of time.

Never one to hesitate, she closed her eyes, and threw caution to the wind, although technically there was no wind, not even a courage-bolstering breeze. Slowly she pulled her blouse from her shoulders, letting it fall to the ground. His gaze lifted to her bare chest and stayed there. The dangerous hunger returned and somewhere in her mind, summer lightning flashed, dazzling her. Just like magic, the breeze began to blow, tossing her caution even further afield.

"You trying to bribe me?" he asked in an unsteady voice.

She smiled, slow and a little unsteady herself. "Is it working?"

Gently he lowered her to the ground, and his mouth took her own. It was a long and hungry kiss that involved grinding tongues and grinding hips, and when his hands touched her brazen nipples, they weren't so gentle, weren't so tender. This was pain, the most beautiful sort of pain. *Desire.* She squeezed her lips shut, silencing her cries, silencing her moans.

He was heavy on top of her, and she could feel him, all of him, thick and throbbing and full of baby-making sperm. Before she could contemplate the consequences even further, he put his mouth to her breast and suckled, pulling hard. Wickedly hard. Her eyes drifted closed, trying not to be too slutty and give away the entire farm, but Gillian was no tease, neither. "Take me."

His fingers moved lower, resting at the zip of her shorts, waiting. "Here?" he said, and there was a dark sin in his eyes that boiled her insides. There were girls who got pregnant, girls who threw away everything for the thrill. Not Gillian.

She laid her hand over his, not in invitation this time.

"Take me to prom," she clarified, not exactly denying the other, but not committing herself to it, either. At least not yet.

Furiously he rolled off her, scrubbing his lean face with his hands. "Goddammit, Gillian. You don't know jack-shit about men. I could die from this sort of pain." Clearly, he was miserable, furious even...so breath-catchingly cute.

Unable to help herself, she started to laugh, embarrassed, awkward, because this was all new to her. Then he started to laugh, and then, thankfully, all the hard anger fell away. Mission accomplished. She wanted to be the temptress. There were few things she couldn't master, but a lifetime of warnings were ringing in her ears, still, there were too many dreams she wanted to live. He made her feel crazy, wild, and while she loved being like that, she knew it wasn't smart.

Feeling better, a little more in control, Gillian pulled on her shirt, and she noticed that he looked relieved, as well. Relieved and much more cooperative, which was a plus since she wasn't ready to give up on her original target just yet.

"You'll take me to the prom? We're seniors and after

this, we gotta be mature with checking accounts and crappy jobs."

At her words, his gaze cooled a bit, because while her great life would be over, his great life was about to start. Maybe after graduation wouldn't be great for him, but it had to be better than life with his father, Frank Hart. She knew Austen was capable of more than working on cars, and tonight, when the pre-graduation clock was ticking, she wanted to know about his post-graduation dreams.

"What are you going to do after May?" she asked, keeping her tone casual.

When he held her in his gaze, she saw something that was a lot more than a car mechanic. Ambition, determination, and she was glad his father hadn't ruined everything for him. "I'm going to go to Austin and then build myself the world's fastest Mustang."

His answer made her smile. 'It's the perfect spot for you."

But while she was smiling, he didn't and slowly it dawned on her that he was leaving. Leaving for good and soon. Not that she shouldn't be surprised, not that she shouldn't be expecting it. Still, she wasn't. "Oh."

He moved closer, reaching out and pushing the hair from her eyes. "Come with me. I'm serious. We can leave this dump and go someplace where there's more excitement than Two-For-One Chicken Fried Steak Night."

Gillian felt a hard rock in her gut. The same sort when she got a B-plus on a test, or when she flubbed her jump during the State cheerleading competition. Exactly the same sort as when a boy told her (as she was sitting there, only moments before trying to be a temptress), that she wasn't worth sticking around for. "Glad to know where I rate."

"This isn't about you, Gilly," he told her and she reminded herself that his world wasn't hers. His nights at home weren't about watching the Cowboys play on Sunday or baking pies for the charity sale. No, his nights weren't nearly so nice.

Everybody knew about the house way back in the empty fields behind town. The beaten-down shack with its peeling gray paint and empty beer cans cluttering up the yard. The oak in the front was more filled with bullet holes than life, and on most nights, angry voices bellowed through the knee-high grass. Angry words from the foul-mouthed, foul-tempered trash that lived there.

At one time, there had been two boys who lived there, but then the eldest went away. Some said he was buried out back, some said he was incarcerated at the State Pen, but nobody knew for sure. And no one ever got a straight answer from either the boy or his father. Misery made Gillian's heart ache for that brother left behind. Hell was supposed to come after death, not before. But he never complained, never talked about it, never showed that it mattered at all.

"I'm sorry," she told him, apologizing for more than her thoughtless words, wishing she could make his situation better.

He touched her forehead, her cheek, cupped her chin in his hand until she had to meet the full-on intensity in his eyes. He had such beautiful eyes. Quicksilver eyes that changed on a dime. Brown and gold melting together, and on a rare occasion, such as this, he would look at you with the full potency of his heart, his soul. A mere woman couldn't help but fall in love.

"Come with me," he said, touching his lips to hers.

He didn't wait for an answer, but kept kissing her, putting a lifetime of kissing into the effort, this boy who never tried too hard at anything, this boy who had failed more than most. Gillian felt a prick of tears at her eyes, because a kiss wasn't supposed to last for an entire lifetime. A kiss was supposed to last until the next minute, the next hour, the next day when she saw him again. A kiss like this meant goodbye.

Goodbye.

There would be no making love, there would be no prom king and queen, there would be no more Austen in her life at all.

The trusting heart was the easiest to break, the hardest to heal, and Gillian was surprised by the pain of it.

"Stay with me," she pleaded, but he lifted his head and she could see him disappearing before her eyes. The boy was no more. Here was the man. Slowly, he shook his head.

She used her shirt to wipe at the tears on her face. Before tonight, she had been so sure of him, of her plans, her dreams. So cock-sure of herself. "I told Mindy you were going to be my date," she confessed, because she told Mindy everything.

"What the hell, Gillian?" His eyes were hot with anger and then something else. She followed his gaze to where her shirt hung open, and she realized that maybe her dreams weren't shot to hell after all.

There was a heaviness in the night air and she could feel the stickiness on her skin. The dark thoughts in her mind should have scared her, but they excited her instead. What did it matter now? He was the only one she wanted. She wanted him to be her first.

Nervously she pushed back the hair from her face—as a woman would, not like a girl.

"Please stay. At least until the prom—"

"God, woman." The words were anguished. Defeated. Sometimes Gillian knew she pressed too hard to get her way, but he wouldn't regret this. She'd make sure of it.

"Is that a yes?" she asked, excitement bubbling through her.

"It's a yes."

With that, she threw herself at him in a shameless fashion, because at least now, they had one more week. A whole seven days that would have to last a lifetime. She didn't want to wait. Not any longer.

Virginity was for fools who thought there would always be tomorrow.

"I love you," she whispered, and he drew back, a surprised expression on his face.

"You don't have to say that."

"I know, but I want to do this right."

He grew still. "Do what right?"

She spread her hands wide, gesturing to the field, the night, the moon. "My first time."

"I thought you and Jeff…"

She shook her head.

"Roger?"

Once more she shook her head.

"Sonny?"

For the last time, she shook her head no. She had thought he'd be pleased, but he didn't look happy about the situation at all.

The wicked light in his eyes dimmed to something more respectable, more honorable. His perfect mouth curled into a heart-stopping grin and she knew that her first time would be exactly as she'd wanted it to be.

"Then we should do this right. Not in a field. Obviously you can't have an up close and personal experience with chiggers in places that chiggers don't belong."

Chiggers?

At that, Gillian stared into the tall grass, seriously considering the ramifications of her virginity-losing decision. Pregnancy, she had considered often enough. Chiggers were something entirely different.

Just the thought of it had her itching behind her knee. Discreetly she scratched.

"We need a humongous bed," he continued on, "because a physically demanding woman like you, well, a man needs room to work, you know? And privacy, no kids, no parents, someplace where nobody can interrupt. And you'll need something better to drink than beer, maybe champagne. And you deserve a whole bucket of flowers. Roses."

Dreamily she smiled up at him because of all the boys she knew, he was the first one to understand the frilly secrets of Gillian's heart.

She'd never seen him like this, so full of ideas and the future, his eyes glittering with excitement. And it was the idea of loving her that brought this big change about. Love truly was a miraculous thing. It could move mountains, it could touch stars and just the thought of it could turn him into the lover she knew he could be.

She brushed at the grass, realizing that his plan sounded a lot more fun than a quick roll in the chiggers. "You want to wait for prom night?"

He nodded, reaching for her shirt and firmly buttoning it closed. "I do."

"Then we wait," she said, feeling a little disappointed, and a little relieved.

With that decided, he took out the old pocket watch

from his jeans and checked the time. "I have to head home."

"I'll see you at school tomorrow?"

"Sure," he said, kissing her first on the nose, and then more urgently on the lips. Then he pulled the watch from his pocket once again. "Here," he told her, handing it to her, his face solemn.

"Why are you giving me this?" she asked, nervous at the seriousness in his voice. "You're going to stay, right?"

He laughed. "For a week. This is for you to count down the time. I can't give you much." He pressed it into her hands. "Take it."

She fingered the worn metal, the scratched glass, and beamed up at him, touched by the gesture. "Really?"

"Sure. Be good."

"Aren't I always?" she asked, not quite as happy about that as she should be. "You're going to rent a tux?"

He glanced over, eyes unblinking. "Sure."

"You'll look nice in a tux. Nearly as good as you'll look without it," she teased.

"You have a very dirty mind," he teased in return. So normal, so happy, so perfect.

"Thank you for noticing."

As he started over the hill, Gillian held the watch close to her heart, and fell back onto the grass, not caring too much about the chiggers at the moment.

Five more days, and then they'd be making love. She should buy some sexy lingerie. Sexy, but not trampy. Maybe white. A soft ecru that matched her skin.

Maybe after that, she could get him to change his mind and stay. A little white lace, some dramatic cleavage. A man's biological urges were a powerful force. She pulled her shirt away from her chest and checked.

Feeling more confident, she silently thanked God for giving her perky tits and a curvy ass that would never go fat.

Prom night. Five days till paradise. And she wanted to make their night together just as special for him as it was going to be for her.

Looking back, she should have realized the truth, but Gillian had never been skilled at reading signs that didn't point in her own fortuitous direction. Five days later, all that changed, but at least then she had someone to blame.

Easy-loving, easy-lying, easy-leaving Austen Hart.

1

BROKEN HEARTS WERE A familiar cause of mayhem in Tin Cup, Texas. Arnold Cervantes had broadsided his girlfriend's F-150 with his riding lawnmower after he learned she'd been stepping out on him with the landscaper. When Doc Emerson filed for divorce, Mrs. Emerson had laced her husband's tapioca pudding with a laxative, a charge that was ultimately overturned by Judge Lansdale, who was the second cousin to the defendant. Oscar Ramirez had flown his wife's plus-sized unmentionables in the Memorial Day parade after she refused him certain sexual favors which Harley considered his right, but which were also illegal according to Texas state law.

In the three years since Gillian Wanamaker had been sworn in as sheriff of Tin Cup, she'd seen a lifetime's worth of passion, foolishness and general human stupidity. In Gillian's humble opinion, people needed to practice more self-control and show a little concern for their own reputation within the community. As a card-carrying member of the Broken Hearts Club herself, Gillian had never been tempted to spray-paint a human being, nor set fire to items of clothing. Or at least, not in a really long time.

Usually Gillian avoided dwelling on past unpleasantries, or those fleeting moments when she had wanted to dig out a fellow human being's heart with a dull nail file, but this morning was different. First she'd stopped at Harley's Five & Dime to sneak a glance at the Austin newspaper, just as she did every day. While checking Thursday's style section, she'd seen the watchful worry in Harley's eyes. Like he expected Gillian to bust out into great heartbroken sobs. Ha. Maybe when she'd been a gauche seventeen, but now? At twenty-seven? Ha. Ha.

Two doors down, at Dot's Good Eats, Dot had been extra nice, giving her a sausage biscuit for free. Free sausage was a soft-hearted act of pity by even the most liberal definition of the word. As if Gillian was someone people felt sorry for. Sorry! She had been crowned Miss Tin Cup four times running. She had been All-State in softball, with a fastball that could kill a man if he wasn't paying attention. Gillian Wanamaker of the San Angelo Wanamakers was a force to be reckoned with, not a pity case. She was an icon, a role model. She was a goddamned institution, much like Lady Bird Johnson, Jackie O, Lady Di and Barbie.

Needing to escape all the sympathetic stares, but without looking as if she needed to, Gillian left the restaurant and headed for the sanctity of the courthouse, where she could cower in peace. Nearly two hundred years ago, they were driving cattle down this street, instead of pick-ups. There was a permanence in Tin Cup, a consistency that Gillian appreciated more than most. As she passed the red-bricked storefronts on Main Street, they were just opening the doors, some of the old-timers shopping before the heat of the day set in. In Texas, if you weren't practical, you didn't survive.

She could see Rita Talleyrand approaching with that "Let's chat" gleam in her eye, so Gillian took the last hundred feet at a fast sprint, cutting across the well-tended lawn, ticking off the landscapers in the process. She waved an apology then darted inside the courthouse, and up the marble steps. The sheriff's office was located on the second floor, and it wasn't fancy or frilly, but it was more than enough. The old wooden desk had served the Tin Cup sheriff since the first world war. The chair creaked when you moved, and had a drunken tilt to the right, but there was a history here, and Gillian was now a part of it. The walls were lined with photos of the dignitaries who had passed through Tin Cup—but never stayed.

Soon all that was going to change with the upcoming Trans-Texas Light Rail line, a four-hour direct route from Austin to Midland via, yes, you heard it here first— Tin Cup.

There were plans for the new station, along with a few extra improvements. A nip and tuck to make Tin Cup, Texas, a travel destination all its own.

After one extra cup of coffee, Gillian settled in her chair, but the mindless paperwork only gave her more time to stew. As she hammered away on the old computer keyboard, she reminded herself that her days were too busy to be filled with ideas of revenge, or physical assault. The Enter key stuck, and she pounded it twice, accidentally cancelling the state's processing form for last month, and she damned every vile participant in this technological conspiracy, along with one non-participant: Austen Hart.

Austen was lumped in merely because he was still

living, breathing and now his personal space was a little closer to Tin Cup and already she could see the tiny prickles breaking out along her skin. Hives, she told herself. Nothing more. Not excitement. No siree, bob.

Gillian leaned back in her chair and inhaled deeply, mainlining oxygen, trying to find her happy place.

She had it all: great job; solid, stable, reliable almost-a-boyfriend; loving family. There was no reason to feel unsatisfied because that would mean she was picky. And Gillian was not picky. Particular, yes. Picky, no.

A loud knocking at her office door interrupted the train-wreck of her thoughts, and Joelle appeared before Gillian had a chance to answer.

"Gillian, your momma is here to see you. She brought the refreshments for the council's lunch meeting, but I don't think the snickerdoodles are going to last until noon. It's the extra chocolate that gets me every time." Joelle slid her hands over well-padded hips and then gave a resigned shrug. "Why aren't you fat? Back in high school, I swore you took up smoking. It was the only logical explanation."

After one blissful sniff, Gillian pushed aside the decadent smell of coconut, chocolate and nuts. "Joelle, how many sit-ups do you see me doing every morning?"

"Three hundred."

"How many miles do I run every afternoon, even when the sidewalks are steaming?"

"Two-point-seven. Twice that, if you get a double-dip at Dot's."

"And how many snickerdoodles do you think I will eat?"

Joelle held her thumb and forefinger an inch apart.

Gillian gave a curt nod. "And do I subject myself to these tortures because I want to?"

"Not unless you have some sort of death wish. Speaking of death wish, the man who shall not be named has got a meeting at the lawyer's tomorrow, and a reservation at the Spotlight Inn for tonight. Late arrival guaranteed by credit card, sometime between six and seven. Delores called first thing this morning. She wanted to know how you'd take the news."

Gillian smiled evenly, calmly, because this information did not faze her. Not at all.

"I'm taking the news fine. Maybe I'll call up Jeff for a date. Maybe we'll rent a room at the Spotlight Inn and moan extra loud."

Joelle wiggled her brows. "I bet he'd like that."

Yeah, Gillian wished that Jeff would like that, but no. "Jeff's too much a gentleman to get a room in town." And that was a good thing, a respectable quality in a man. Definitely a good thing. *Definitely.*

"I was talking about Austen," Joelle replied, a disgustingly knowing glare in her eyes.

"Can we not?"

"You want an extra snickerdoodle before I tell your mom you're available?"

Gillian scanned the While You Were Out Messages piled neatly on her desk. Mindy had called. Five times. Mindy—who used to be Mindy Lansdale and was now Mrs. Mindy Shuck—would have heard the news about the man who shall not be named. She would want an update. Ever since second grade, Mindy had been Gillian's best friend and knew all of her secrets. Mindy would understand the misery that Gillian was going through and would want Gillian to discuss it in tortuous detail. Gillian couldn't call. Not yet. Did Jackie O whine about the miseries of her love life? No way.

As she pondered how best to avoid her best friend

without seeming as if she was avoiding her best friend, the decadent aroma of chocolate and coconut lingered in the air, like a siren's call that would give her the sugar-high that she'd need to get through this day. Realizing there wasn't enough sugar on the planet to get her through this day, Gillian sighed. "Bring two cookies."

"You're going to do five miles?" Joelle asked in her sweetest, most polite voice.

In answer, Gillian massaged her temple with her middle finger. Joelle, never dumb, left four snickerdoodles on the desk. Gillian would have to run six miles, but it was worth it. Two seconds later, her mother muscled in.

"I came as soon as Vernelle told me. How are you feeling?" Modine Wanamaker put a warm hand on her daughter's forehead. "You look a little flushed, but no fever."

Gently Gillian moved her mother's hand and tried to appear relaxed. "I'm fine, Momma."

Gillian's mother was a short dumpling of a woman, with a perpetual smile, which never wavered except for a small flash of disapproval when she witnessed her only daughter dressed in a regulation uniform with boots to match.

It was a sad fact that Gillian's law enforcement career conflicted with Modine's life goals for Gillian. Gillian's mother respected the law and admired it, but like many other things, she didn't want her only daughter doing it in case it interfered with Gillian's grandkid-making ability. Three cross-stitched birth announcements sat near the top of Modine's needlework bag, almost ready for framing. All that was missing were the names and birth dates.

Gillian always pretended she never saw them. Modine

knew she had. But they smiled and loved each other anyway because that was what mothers and daughters did.

Now Modine took a step back and gave her daughter the once-over. "I told Vernelle there was nothing to worry about from that Hart boy. I told her you'd forgiven him."

"I haven't forgiven him, Momma. He ditched me at prom with no phone call, no letter. I had a new dress. I was elected Prom Queen."

He was supposed to be my first.

"And in the end, look at how much better your life is without him," her mother reminded her. "Frank Hart, bless his black heart, raised two misbegotten boys, and those sorts of doings put a dark shadow on the soul. The life of crime, the drugs. Certainly we have to provide for the unfortunate, but there's nowhere in the good book that says you have to marry them. Besides, you have Jeff, who was raised proper and with the right sorts of values and respect for his fellow man. Vernelle let it slip that he was looking at diamonds. Anything I should know?" Her brows shot up, silently demanding confirmation in that way mothers had when they suspected their daughters were keeping secrets. Sure, Gillian had her secrets, but this wasn't one of them.

Gillian shook her head. "Nothing to say." Inwardly, though, she frowned at the thought of diamonds. She liked Jeff, he was fun and thoughtful, the salt of the earth. A vet. The man who healed all of God's smallest and most helpless creatures, but...

Why did there have to be a but? There shouldn't be a but. But there was a but.

No doubt, she was picky. Frankly, if she ever found

happiness, it would be more than such a persnickety McFickle deserved.

No, that was negative thinking, and Gillian did not believe in negative thinking. Not ever. Not feeling the need to continue the conversation, Gillian huddled over the office printer. While she collected the last pages of the state's processing forms, her mother pulled at the container of paper clips on her desk, bending each one this way and that before twisting three into a flower. Gillian sighed, but her mother, accustomed to Gillian's particular nature, ignored her. "There's a rummage sale at the church on Saturday and I'm putting together some boxes. You have any clothes you want to get rid of?"

There was one slinky white nightgown, never used, still sitting at the back of her closet. It would be perfect for some deserving female who couldn't afford something pretty.

"I got nothing, Momma." Not only picky, but selfish, too. She started to restore her paper clips to their proper place, but then thought better of it, removing her hand from the magnetic container. Metal conducted electricity, and who knew when lightning might strike within a brick-enclosed building.

"Surely you have something to give, Gilly." Modine Wanamaker firmly believed that the road to heaven was paved with dramatic acts of Christian charity. It was a doctrine not without its problems. Six years ago, Gillian's mother had given away the farm. Technically, it had been a two-story Colonial on two acres, which Modine had donated to the poor unfortunate Taylor family when they lost their house to the bank. The next morning, Gillian's parents had shown up on her doorstep, claiming there was plenty of room at her house.

And how did you kick out your own parents?

You didn't.

Yes, Gillian was picky and selfish, but nothing trumped blood-relations in her mind. The way Gillian saw it, having her parents shack up with her was penance for not only everything bad she'd done prior, but an insurance policy against future acts of badness, as well. Her mother's worried expression tugged at Gillian's heartstrings. No, nothing could trump blood-relations in the cardiac region, either. She blew out a dramatic sigh, just like any unworthy daughter would. "I'll see what I can find."

Relieved that her only daughter was no longer going to hell, Modine began to poke through Gillian's phone messages, until Gillian stopped her with a firm hand.

Her mother's serene expression never wavered, and sometimes Gillian wished that her own nature was a little more...*forgiving.* "I'm cooking King Ranch Chicken for supper. Your favorite."

"I've got a meeting with Wayne over at the Chamber of Commerce. He's wasn't happy with the security for the Fourth of July last year. A twenty-five percent drop in business because the sidewalks were locked down. I've got constituents, Momma. I'm an elected official who lives and dies by the voters of this town. The chicken will have to wait."

Gillian made a mental note to call Wayne as soon as her mother left. If she did that, then it wasn't exactly lying, more anticipating what she should have done anyway.

"Can't you leave that sort of business to the mayor?"

Gillian stared silently. Leroy Parson was the mayor of Tin Cup, a ninety-three-year-old war hero from WWII. On every Memorial Day, Veteran's Day and the Fourth of July, Leroy led the usual parade, but that was pretty much the only time that Leroy showed up for work. Nobody was willing to oust a war hero, so instead the town was waiting for him to kick the bucket, leaving Gillian pretty much the top bureaucrat in charge—which her mother considered one more roadblock in the way of her future baby-making.

In the end, Modine knew she was beat. "I'll leave you a plate in the fridge," she said. "Don't be home too late. You know the grapevine in this town. They'll have you pregnant and on a nine-month trip to Europe before you can say Hester…Hester… Well, never you mind what the name is. You know it's that woman from the *Scarlet Letter.*"

"This is the twenty-first century, Momma. We're not all living in medieval times."

Her mother clucked her tongue. "Never underestimate the power of reputation. It can shame a woman, it can make a woman. In the dark ages, they had stonings. Now they have Facebook."

Gillian shot her mother an innocent look. "I thought the internet was the work of the devil."

"Certainly not. I found the best recipe site…" She stopped the moment she caught on to Gillian's tricks. "I will not be sidetracked. It's time Jeff Junior made an honest woman out of you, Gillian. I was married when I was seventeen, your grandmother married when she was fourteen."

"Good thing I wasn't sheriff then, or I'd have to arrest Grandpa Charlie for it. Thank you for the snickerdoodles, Momma. The council always loves it when you feed them."

"There's a plate without nuts for Martin. See you at the house. And don't stay out too late." With that, her mother was gone, and peace and sanity were once more restored.

Fortunately, the rest of the day passed quietly. One arrest for shoplifting, one hour spent promising Wayne that in lieu of barricades, the town would provide two extra officers for this year's holiday celebrations. In the afternoon, they'd retrieved one would-be runaway, twelve-year-old Aaron Metzger who was found hiding in his neighbor's garage. The last item on her calendar, the town council meeting, had ended on a sour note, because nobody wanted to hire the mayor's good-for-nothing great-grand-nephew to build the new train station, although no one wanted to tell the mayor either. All in all, an ordinary day in town, and not a further word about Austen Hart, not that she was bothered by that. Not at all.

She hadn't expected a big to-do. She hadn't expected a phone call from the man. Not at all.

Frowning, Gillian looked at the clock, and decided that half past seven was late enough. Time to go home, spend some quality time with her mom and dad and convince her parents that her insides weren't twisted in nervous knots because the perpetrator of Gillian's Worst Day Ever was back in town.

She had almost finished organizing a few reports in her messenger bag, when Joelle burst through the door, cheeks flushed, eyes sparkling with criminal intent. "Got a nine-one-one call from Delores. Kids are throwing eggs at passing cars on the interstate, right outside the Spotlight Inn."

Gillian frowned because there were no egg-throwers in Tin Cup. There were paint-sprayers, there were turkey-tossers, there were Silly-Stringers, but not egg-throwers. Everybody knew that the Texas heat fried the eggs before they could do any damage. "Sounds vaguely suspicious," she murmured, continuing to organize the contents of her bag.

"I only take the calls." Joelle shrugged, not bothering to dispute the suspicious part.

Gillian drummed her nails on the desk. "Can you get a patrolman out there?"

"You want Martin to take it? You know it's their anniversary. They're headed for San Angelo for the night."

Gillian's frown deepened. "And I bet Delores knew that."

"Everybody knew that, Gilly."

"She hates me."

"She wanted head cheerleader. You're going to pay for that for the rest of your life."

"Fine," snapped Gillian, quelling the flicker of excitement in her gut. "Can you put out a call from dispatch, saying that I'll be on patrol?"

"You got it. Five-oh on the scene."

"This isn't Hawaii, Jo."

"Sorry. Sometimes I get caught up in the drama," muttered Joelle as she fussed with her curls, now having been put in her place, and making Gillian feel like a heel in the process. Life had been a lot easier when Gillian didn't have to worry about whether other people thought she was a bitch or not. High school had been all about being the alpha girl, the top dog, the queen bee. When Austen had left town, everyone snickered, because then she was only the alpha girl who'd been ingloriously dumped. That was one trend that nobody wanted to follow. Jackie O had never been dumped.

Gillian gave Joelle an uneasy smile. "Dano, put out the call."

Joelle grinned, good spirits back in place. "That's a big ten-four, boss."

Pushing back from her desk, Gillian slipped on the dark sunglasses and checked herself in the mirror. Khaki wasn't her best color, it washed out the blond of her hair, but the tiny handcuffs pin at the collar was a nice touch.

These days she carried a Glock 19 instead of pom-poms, and wore a sheriff's star-studded uniform instead of the blue-and-white tank top miniskirt of the Tin Cup Lionettes. Her hair was a foot shorter, too. Now, she had a nice sensible bob that fell a few inches below her shoulders. No way would Austen recognize her in a regulation brown, cotton-polyester blend.

No, the princessy Gillian Wanamaker had disappeared forever. She patted the revolver at her hip. Hot, armed and dangerous. Just the way God had intended women to be.

2

THE SPOTLIGHT INN WAS on Interstate 78, just behind the orange-and-white stripes of WhataBurger. The hotel was far enough from town that cars would not be spotted in the parking lot. It was close enough to town that those that weren't smart enough to park their cars behind the hotel would most likely get noticed by the UPS man, who was close friends with the receptionist at the *Tin Cup Gazette*, who also served as a deacon at First Baptist on Sundays. People joked about six degrees of separation, but in Tin Cup, one degree of separation was usually overstating the truth.

As Gillian pulled into the front drive, the sun was disappearing beneath the horizon, casting a red tint to the sky. The dusky heat was still a killer, waves of it rising from the concrete and making everything look hazy and surreal. In the movies, when the world shimmered, it signaled a trip to the past, but when summer hit Tin Cup, the world was in permanent shimmer, a town not ready to give up its past, while simultaneously trying to grab hold of the future. It was a dilemma that Gillian understood well.

It wasn't exactly that she wanted to see Austen, she

told herself as she poked around outside, looking for egg-shells, egg-streaked road signs or any other indication that somebody was egg-spressly messing with her town. It was more that she wanted to see Austen in order to finally write him out of her life.

For ten sweat-pouring minutes, she wandered outside the hotel, searching for evidence, but now all she had was frizzy hair, dusty boots and the sure knowledge that something was rotten in Tin Cup, and it wasn't the mysteriously disappearing eggs. Feeling cranky, she chose to blame Austen Hart because if he wasn't in town, nobody would be messing with her.

Maybe the myth of the man was bigger than the reality, she thought optimistically as she headed toward the motel's covered entrance. If there was a lick of justice in the world, he would have a spare tire around his middle, and his hairline would be four inches behind the crown of his head.

A trucker roared by and sat on his horn and Gillian waved in response, before pushing her sunglasses on top of her hair. At the very least, the man could have written her a note to explain his actions. Another memento that she could have kept buried back in her closet. It was that sort of what-if thinking that made it hard to forget him. Hard to forget the too short nights spent star-gazing together on Peterson's Ridge. Hard to forget the way he would twist her hair around his finger and then pull her close for a kiss.

Even Jeff, perfect, perfect Jeff, couldn't affect her the way a mere boy had. There were prickles on her arms again, and furiously she rubbed at them until they disappeared because she was too smart to get stupid again.

Before she confronted Delores, she double-checked her reflection in the glass doors, making sure the hair was in place, making sure the mascara looked fabulous, making sure that Gillian was still the most well-put-together female in three counties. When she was satisfied with the face looking back at her, she pulled open the doors and strolled inside. Casual. Easy. Confident.

"Didi! Look at you," she purred in her best-friends-forever voice. "I love what you've done with your hair. Something new?"

Delores Hancock was twenty-seven, the same age as Gillian, and had a husband of ten years, two kids and had presided over the front desk at the Spotlight Inn since her great-uncle Hadley had died near eight years back. Her hair was glossy black, coordinating nicely with the snapping dark eyes that were particularly pretty when she wore a little extra liner.

Unlike Gillian, who knew the value of a wide smile—fake or otherwise—Delores could never mask her appreciation of a compliment—fake or otherwise—and some of the sharpness faded from her eyes.

"Thank you for noticing. I had it blown out yesterday, but Bobby hadn't said a word."

Gillian's smile relaxed a bit. "Men don't care about good hair, or dirty dishes. All they want is a piece of tail and a cold beer on Sundays. You can't hold him responsible for something that's not part of his DNA."

"God's truth, honey," Delores agreed, but then shot her a smile that was a little too sugary. Joelle was right. Delores was going to hate her for the rest of her life.

Abandoning the token attempt at an olive branch, Gillian leaned in on the counter, one shoulder cocked low. It was a move that she'd seen in a lot of old Westerns, and Gillian used it whenever she needed to act rugged. "So tell me about those kids. I nosed around outside, but didn't see any sign of them, broken-egg yolks or splattered cars."

"I cleaned it all up," Delores answered quickly. A little too quickly.

"Really? And none of the irate drivers stuck around?"

"Would you stick around this place?" Delores asked, nodding toward the wide stretch of highway and the exit sign that was still spray painted over with ODESSA-PERMIAN SUCKS, exactly as it had been since before Gillian was born.

"Got a point. Did you get a look at the kids involved?"

"No. The sun was right there in my eyes. I think they were wearing T-shirts, jeans and UT ball caps."

Which described 99.7 percent of the juveniles in most of the state. "Sounds like we got us a mystery," murmured Gillian, not wanting to call Delores a liar, which wouldn't further what could turn into a beautiful friendship.

Delores stared at the door, a cat-and-the-canary smile on her face, and Gillian froze because the prickles had returned. "My, my, my..." said Delores softly.

Gillian instantly pushed her glasses down over her eyes and forced herself to move away from the security of the counter. "I'll get back with you about those pesky kids."

Slowly she moved toward the door, her face expressionless, pretending to ignore the man who had just walked in with his easy way and knowing smile.

Three more steps and then she would be past him.

Two.

One.

At last the door was directly in front of her, and she

pushed at it with unsteady hands. There was no one to notice the slight tremors…except for him.

One steady hand beat her to it, tanned skin, long fingers, conspicuously clean nails. "Thank you," she told him, eyes straight ahead, ignoring the faint whiff of some expensive cologne.

"You shouldn't have cut your hair," he answered in a low voice meant for her ears alone. The husky sound created a long-forgotten spark, a flash of summer lightning that she thought she'd buried for good.

Gillian didn't bother to reply; wasn't sure if she could. Her heart was hammering too loud in her chest. Head high, she strode toward the sheriff's cruiser, and a mere four lifetimes later she had recovered her composure. With a hard foot on the accelerator, she gunned the engine, and was driving away.

Away from Delores, away from the Spotlight Inn and away from the man who had grown up to be a long, hot mess of temptation. But Gillian was stronger than that.

If this town wanted entertainment, then by God, they were going to have to spring for HBO.

AUSTEN HART HAD spent the last ten years dreaming of Gillian Wanamaker. Over that long a span, a man could create elaborate ideals of a woman—or fantasies, if he wanted to call a spade a spade. In his mind, her mouth had always been wide, perfectly glossed with rosebud pink. Her blond hair had always fallen in long, silky rolls down her back. In his mind, everything about her had always been mouth-watering perfection.

Unfortunately, Austen had never been much of a perfectionist. "Good enough" had served him well, and sometimes "not a chance in hell" seemed most appropriate. But that didn't stop him from dreaming. He quit staring at the glass door and told himself, "Not a chance in hell."

Today she seemed different. Harder in a lot of ways, although that could be the gun at her hip.

Damn. That was one career he would have never expected. Sheriff, he thought, remembering the badge. There were men who thought a woman packing heat was sexy. Austen had a healthy respect for the power of a gun. He'd been on the wrong end of one way too many times to be turned on, but Gillian...

Mmm-mmm.

The clerk coughed to clear her throat, and Austen smiled automatically.

Normally, Austen didn't mind being the object of attention. Hell, these days, he sought it out. Life of the party. Seeker of the limelight. Man of the hour.

Normally, he didn't mind knowing that everyone was watching, but not in this town. Everyone here lived and died by their family, and Austen had always wanted that, too. Family, connections, solidity. But for the Harts? Ha. That was a laugh.

His older brother, Tyler, had left as soon as he could. Their mother had disappeared—no, she had deserted them, he corrected. He had a sister, Brooke—a sister he'd never known until recently and wasn't sure he wanted to. No, the Harts should have been a family, but somehow, it'd gotten all screwed up. Gee, thanks, Frank.

When Tyler had gotten a full scholarship to college—two-hundred long miles away in Houston—that meant all eyes in Tin Cup were watching Austen. They were waiting for him to follow in his father's footsteps. To explode in a violent rage, or stash a few purloined dollars in his pocket, or yell obscenities at any female that walked by—just like Frank Hart used to do. Six to sixty, coed to grandmother, his father hadn't been a discerning man.

Austen had never liked the eyes watching him, judging him. He didn't have Tyler's brains, Tyler's ability to shut everything out. So Austen had done what he could; when that didn't work, he ran, possibly committing a class C felony in the process—as rumored around Tin Cup, where folks liked to believe the worst of the Hart family. Once he'd gotten the hell out of town, the air was a little clearer, and eventually Austen had made a quasi-respectable name for himself in the state's capital.

The receptionist at the desk was Delores Somebody, a girl who had flirted with him in high school. Most girls did at one time or another. It was a rite of passage: hurling spitballs at the principal, cheating on a math exam and screwing Austen Hart. Most adolescent males wouldn't mind that part, would have actively encouraged it. Yes, Austen had actively encouraged it, but he had minded it, too. A Hart was late-night material, the 2:00 a.m. phone call on a Saturday night. Everybody knew it except for Gillian, who thought she had the power to change it all.

Yeah, right.

"When are you checking out?" Delores asked, nodding to the small bag he had packed, her eyes still a little flirty.

"Tomorrow." 9:30 a.m. to be exact. As soon as the papers were signed. After that, Austen would disappear from this town once again. He ran his fingers over the fresh daisies on the counter, simply because he could. Simply because there was no one to look at him sideways anymore, no one to follow him around in the stores.

"That was Gillian Wanamaker you passed on the way in."

"No kidding?" he said, sliding his sunglasses into the suit pocket. "She's changed."

"Not so much. Still thinks she runs this town."

Austen hid his smile. Knowing Gillian, she probably did. "I'll grab my stuff and be out of your hair." With a polite nod, he collected the room key and picked up his bag, heading for the privacy of his room.

Her laughter caught him from behind, and Austen forced himself to slow down, walk easy. "No bother," she called out. "It's been a slow day. You should hit the night life. Get a beer at Smitty's. There's a lot of people who would like to see you again."

"Maybe," he lied.

A few minutes later, he had kicked off his boots and taken a shower, scrubbing off the dust of the road. The room was a clean, serviceable yellow, with a king-sized bed, a wall-mounted TV and a wide variety of flyers that extolled the virtues of Tin Cup, Texas: a modern recreation of Texas past. After reading a few pages, Austen put the booklets back in their place. In the ten years since he'd been gone, they'd built a new bank, a library, four churches and a ball field.

Golly, gee willikers, Wally.

That had been the hardest thing about Tin Cup, the consistency. Feeling not so much like a tourist, Austen stretched on the bed, closing his eyes, because he didn't care, he didn't have to care. It was in the middle of all that not caring when his cell rang.

"Hey, honey. Missing me yet?"

Carolyn Carver was the governor's oldest daughter, and as such had a high opinion of her own importance. As Austen was a state lobbyist, her opinion wasn't too far off. The cell connection was rotten, so Austen moved to the window where the static cleared. "I just got here, just walked in the door. I think I'm going to kick up my feet, and watch the cow tipping from my window."

West Texas wasn't a land for the faint of heart. It was hot and brutal and flat, an endless landscape of scrubby oak trees, dotted with the oil pumping units, their metallic heads bobbing up and down, feeding off the earth.

"When you coming home?" Carolyn asked. He'd been seeing her off and on for almost a year, and managed their relationship carefully. Austen wasn't going to get serious with Carolyn, and she knew that, but he wasn't going to make her mad, either.

"Shelby can do one-fifty when pressed, but I'd better play it safe. You know these country cops and the speed traps."

"You can tell them it's a state emergency. Tell them that Carolyn Carver wants to get laid."

He laughed aloud because he knew she expected him to. "You keep that thought, and I'll be back before you know it."

"Maggie Patterson called looking for you. Said she was hoping to catch you before you left. Did she call your cell?"

"No."

"Well, she said you couldn't do anything from out there, anyway."

"What did she need?"

"Some kid in the after-school program got arrested, and you've been duly appointed to bail him out, or talk him out, or bust him out. I swear, if her husband wasn't your boss…"

Austen frowned. There wasn't a hell of a lot he could

do remotely, but maybe... "I'll give her a call. See what she's got on her hands."

"A hard knock in the head from a crew of gang-bangers who know how to hot-wire a car, that's what she's going to have on her hands if she's not careful."

Austen didn't even flinch. "Your father's tough on crime. It'll look good on his campaign posters."

Carolyn giggled because in her world she wouldn't know how to hotwire a battery. But Austen did.

"There's a new band playing at Antone's tonight. Jack Haywood doesn't want to go alone."

"Jack's an okay guy, but don't let him make you pay for dinner. That boy doesn't have any class at all."

She laughed again, and he moved toward the bed, hearing the reception go spotty. "Listen, Carolyn, I'm having trouble with the lines out here. Gotta go," he told her, and then hung up, letting himself breathe.

Once again, he sacked out on the bed, but the curtains were half-open, letting him see to the outside, letting him see exactly what nothingness was putting the sweat on his neck. Idiot, that's what he was. He moved to the window, and pushed back the sheers, and gazed out on the land. His shoulders ached from the drive, and he rolled them back, slowing his pulse, embracing the calm.

Why did he let the ghost of Frank Hart get to him? Why did he let this town crawl under his skin? Because it was who he was.

He picked up his cell, called Maggie only to find out that L.T., one of the boys in the program, had gone for a joyride. Maggie's afterschool program was her pride and joy, but criminal activities always put a damper on its fundraising, so Austen did what he always did and promised to clean up the mess. Quietly, of course, and then he called Captain Juarez of the Austin P.D. After promising that L.T. would attend one weekend of Youth Corps Training and then sweetening the deal with a few seats to the Longhorns' home opener for the captain's trouble, Austen called Maggie and let her know that L.T. had been sprung.

One more delinquent back on the street. In Austen's expert opinion, sure, you could put lipstick on a pig, but no matter how much you tried, it's still a pig, and before long, that pig is going to end up being cooked and served up for breakfast, alongside scrambled eggs and a hot cup of coffee.

The next moment, he heard a discreet tap on the door. There wasn't room service at the Spotlight Inn, and he hoped to God it wasn't the cops…

Unless it was Gillian.

Not a chance in hell, answer the damned door.

It was Delores, still wearing the same flirty smile, only now it looked apologetic, as well. "I know that I shouldn't be here, but Gillian called to check up on things, which I know wasn't the truth, but during the conversation, she let it slip that she was going to Smitty's—not that she wasn't being completely obvious because the girl doesn't have a subtle bone in her body, and I almost didn't tell you—"

Delores took a breath. "—but I decided I should, because, even though it's not my place to poke my nose where it doesn't belong, I thought, what if she's there, and you're not, and everybody thinks poorly of you because you're not, and then I'd have to live with the guilt of my actions. In the end, I just couldn't do it."

Austen stared flatly, tempted to feign illness, maybe the ebola virus, but no. Sure, he was being played like a cheap violin, but he still wanted to go. He wanted to see Gillian again.

"I'll think about it."

He thought about it for a long seven and a half minutes before his mind was made up. He changed into something a little nicer, washed his hands and polished his boots, and then left the safety of his room behind him.

Delores was still at the front desk, reading from the latest issue of *People*, and Austen strolled past like a man with no place to go, and no woman to see. "You know, I've changed my mind. Smitty's, huh? I remember that place. Still over behind the Texaco?"

"Hasn't moved. Landry's still tending bar, and she gets cranky if you don't laugh at her jokes. Been known to cut off more than one man for not showing proper appreciation for the entertainment. Such as it is."

"Thanks for the tip. I'll be careful. Lots of people there on a Thursday?"

"Everybody in town," she promised, and as he walked away, he could hear Delores picking up the phone and starting to dial. In less than ten minutes, everybody would know exactly where he was, including Gillian.

Austen suspected that he was putting lipstick on a pig. In fact, considering the way he had left Tin Cup, Texas, he suspected that he was going to end up on a plate, served alongside scrambled eggs and a hot cup of coffee.

And yet still he walked out into the night.

Some things never changed.

3

THERE WAS AN ART to a world-class meringue. It required patience and control. The egg whites had to be whipped to an exact stiffness, the peaks had to be swirled with artistic precision. The toppings were spread on the chocolate cream pie with care, just waiting for Gillian to finish her masterpiece. The spatula was poised in midair, ready to rewrite culinary history, when Mindy burst in through the back door.

"You shouldn't break in on a sheriff. I could shoot you dead and there's no judge in the state that will convict me."

Mindy took a long look at the pie, and shook her head, grabbing the spatula from Gillian's hand. With a merciless smile, she began to massacre what had been a work of art.

"Give me a break. No criminal is going to bust in through the kitchen door," Mindy insisted. "Emmett Wanamaker is usually out playing poker in his garage. Modine Wanamaker is usually found in the kitchen and Gillian Wanamaker is never one to be taken by surprise."

Not anymore, thought Gillian to herself. "Why are

you here?" she asked, thinking seriously about pulling the spatula away, but that was exactly what Mindy wanted.

"Are you going to go?" her former best friend asked.

Gillian pretended ignorance and poured two glasses of water from the pitcher on the counter. If Mindy wasn't seven months pregnant, Gillian would have opted for wine. In fact, if she was a lesser friend, she would have poured herself wine, and made Mindy suffer with water. But she was a world-class friend, a world-class baker, a world-class basket case. After downing her glass, Gillian eyed the lopsided meringue. Unable to restrain herself, she grabbed the spatula out of Mindy's hand.

Mindy checked her watch and laughed. "Three minutes. That's a new record."

"Eat this," she shot back, adjusting the balance of the topping, putting the swirls back in their rightful place.

"You're baking."

Gillian looked up and glared. "So?"

"You've heard. You're in culinary denial."

"I can bake without an ulterior motive. It's not a crime. I would know."

Mindy, damn her best-friended-ness, shot her a skeptical look. "You need to go."

Undeterred, Gillian put the pie on the windowsill and started work on the next one.

"How many are you making?" Mindy asked.

"Seven," Gillian muttered under her breath.

Mindy only whistled.

Gillian straightened, then scowled. "Are you going to stand there with your baby-momma smirk, or are you going to help? And no, that does not mean you can touch my meringue. Grab the bluebonnet tray from above the…"

Gillian never finished. Mindy's head was already buried in the cabinet next to the stove. "You have to go," Mindy insisted, sliding the tray on the white-tiled counter. Gillian had laid the tile herself, and painted the backsplash with a daisy-chain of flowers. She studied the grout with a critical eye. It was dingy, needing to be cleaned. Tonight, she could do that. And laundry. Maybe scrub the bathroom floors, as well. *Compulsive? Nah.*

"Don't wimp out now,"

"I can't hear you," Gillian answered loudly, so loudly that her mother poked her head in through the swinging kitchen door.

"Gillian?" she asked, and then spotted Mindy, and *of course,* had to lavish Mindy with a big, squeezy hug, not wise to the sadistic machinations in Mindy's hormonally overcharged heart. "Mindy! Didn't hear you come in, but when Emmett's got the air conditioner running on high, I can't hear a darn thing. Look at you," she purred, standing back and assessing Mindy's belly with a grandmotherly eye.

Then, just as they all knew she would, she turned to her daughter, shook her head once, and walked out of the room in heartbroken silence.

"You didn't have to wear the pink checks," Gillian pointed out, nodding at Mindy's adorable maternity blouse in estrogen-exploding pink.

Mindy grinned. "Never underestimate the impact of your wardrobe decision."

"What bubblehead said that?"

"You did," Mindy reminded her cheerfully. "What are you going to wear?"

"I'm not going," Gillian answered, spelling out vulgar words in the meringue and then swirling over them.

"You have to go. Think of your pride, your upstanding reputation with all the women in this town. You're our Che Guevara, our Davy Crockett, our Gloria Steinem. Take pity on those of us who have succumbed to the bonds of marriage. We need your strength, your unsinkable spirit. Gillian Wanamaker cowers from no man, least of all this one. Do you want him to think that you are too yellow-bellied to see him again? If you can't do it for yourself, think of the women of Tin Cup, Gillian. Think of us, the faceless, the nameless, the married."

Gillian couldn't help but smile. She placed the pie on the breakfast table and pulled the next one from the refrigerator. "He doesn't even know that I know where he is."

"Oh, sure, Sherlock. Riddle me this. How do we know that he's going to be at Smitty's?"

"Delores told Bobby, who told the doc, who told your mother," Gillian explained in her patient voice.

"Exactly! And how did Delores ascertain this intriguing fact?"

Gillian knew where this conversation was leading. She had thought through the paces herself, not that she'd ever admit it. "Delores knew because *apparently* he conversed with her and told her."

"And do you think he would have conversed with her and let that piece of information loose unless he knew in the bowels of his black heart that it would get back to you? That conversation was no mere tongue-slip. It was a master plan, a public challenge, a gauntlet. If you don't show up, then everybody will know that you know and decided to stay home alone. Once again."

It was a cold reminder of Prom Night, when Gillian

had stayed home alone, rather than endure the snickers. "I could have plans," Gillian answered, more than a little defensively.

"Except that when Jeff called, you turned him down, ergo, everybody knows you don't have plans."

Gillian picked up the spatula and carved little daggers into the topping. "Maybe I don't want to go to a bar."

"Maybe," agreed Mindy, "but that's not what everybody is going to be thinking. You know what they're going to think? They're going to look at Gillian Wanamaker, the former pride of Crockett County, the only female to take blue ribbons in both baking and marksmanship, and they are going to feel sorry for her. They're going to think that Gillian Wanamaker has gone soft."

"I have not," Gillian shot back.

"Then you have to go."

Mindy was right. Gillian would be branded a coward, held up for ridicule—again. Sighing, she spun the pie around and started on the other side of the meringue. "You think he did this all to force my hand? Make me show up?" Gillian didn't want to read things into the situation. She didn't want to spend three hours analyzing the Austen Hart mind. Most of all, she didn't want to make chocolate cream pies. Fat and flustered, all because of a man who wasn't worth the calories. Dammit.

"Of course he did it to make you show up. It's the way his mind thinks now. Assuming the worst about human behaviors. Assuming that greed will overcome statesmanship, that cowardice will triumph over bravery. And that's not even taking into account rumors of his impending indictment. It's the treacherous mind of a lobbyist."

"Or someone who spends too much time watching

soap operas," Gillian added, putting the next pie on the counter.

Mindy was not deterred. "It's the way you used to think. I used to admire you. You used to be the queen of sneaky."

Gillian allowed herself a smile. "Maybe I still am."

"So you're going to go? I'll go with you."

Gillian took a long glance at Mindy's swelling belly covered by the pink-ruffled maternity top. "You can't drink."

"Smitty's serves more than beer. I'll order me a Shirley Temple and give you the cherry in case you need an extra one."

Gillian whacked her on the arm, but knew she'd been out-snookered…but only because she chose to be out-snookered. It was true. Gillian Wanamaker cowered for no man. "He looked good."

"So tell me about it. Still hot?" Mindy asked, resting on the counter with a leer.

"Hotter," replied Gillian, because she did have a reputation and responsibility and she took her role-model duties seriously. Well, that, and he did look good.

"How's the hair? He had great hair."

"It's still a little wild. Longer than what an Eagle Scout wears, but it's very…touchable."

"Did he say anything?"

"He told me I shouldn't have cut my hair."

Mindy nodded. "It was the pigtails in the cheerleader outfit. It was more porn than wholesome."

"Says who?"

"Says you."

They both smiled and Gillian wasn't even upset when Mindy stuck her finger in the pie, drilling through meringue to the rich chocolate below. Most everybody else went for the surface topping, but not Mindy. She knew that the best was what was inside. So did Gillian. It was the reason they were friends.

"I miss those days," Gillian admitted with a sigh.

"Late nights, hand jobs and drinking behind the Piggly Wiggly?"

"I wish. Then I wouldn't feel so old." Mindy and Gillian had always held back, always played by the rules, until their first year in community college when Mindy had met her future husband, Brad. Immediately thereafter, Mindy had moved to the dark side and left Gillian alone.

"Wait until you have to buy yourself some stretchmark cream," teased Mindy. "Then talk to me about getting old." Gillian watched as Mindy pulled another pie from the refrigerator, closing it with the swell of her stomach.

"You're not getting old. You're carrying a bowling ball on top of your privates. It's not natural."

"How long are you going to stall in the kitchen? The town is waiting. It's Austen vs. Gillian: The R-Rated Years."

"I don't want to see him."

"You wouldn't be making seven chocolate cream pies if you didn't want to see him."

"He's pond scum."

"He's a first-class son of a bitch. He's a Hart. You want him. Trust me, it's a female thing."

"I don't want to be stupid."

"It's only stupid if your heart gets smashed up against the rocks. Crush him under your heel, and then—" Mindy lowered her voice "—you have sex with him."

"Why?" asked Gillian, morbidly curious.

"What happens if you don't?"

"I go home."

"What happens if you do?"

And then Gillian saw the track of Mindy's more salacious thoughts. If Gillian slept with Austen, then she'd never have the fantasy playing in her head again. Never have the feeling of girl, interrupted, not anymore. Never feel like she'd had something good ripped away. This would just be a man, a woman and a bar. It was cheap and tawdry, nothing magical or romantic at all. It would be perfect. Gillian took stock of Mindy, who was silently waiting for her to see the brilliance of the idea. And she did. In fact, it was so brilliant that Gillian should have thought of it herself. She was the brains in the friendship, not Mindy. Maybe pregnancy had done something to Mindy's brain, made her smarter, wiser.

But still carrying a large bowling ball on top of her privates.

Feeling better and more in control, Gillian dragged Mindy upstairs, where Gillian began to methodically inspect and reject the contents of her closet.

Finally, Gillian hit on The Perfect Outfit, and held up the shirt to the mirror, examining herself with a critical eye. "What do you think? The black silk unbuttoned two buttons, but not three, paired with the Gucci skirt and the Jimmy Choos."

Mindy rolled her eyes. "You don't own a pair of Jimmy Choos."

"They look just like them," Gillian answered, holding up the shoes as proof, pleased to see the stunned admiration in Mindy's eyes.

"No! Where did you get 'em?"

"Ebay."

"Shopping online so that no one knows the actual

brand," Mindy breathed, seeing the beauty of Gillian's secrets. "The queen of sneak, yes, indeed."

"Never underestimate the impact of your wardrobe decisions," she stated calmly, but inside, her heart was ready to explode. This was about pride, she reminded herself. This was about correcting history and making Austen Hart know exactly what he missed out on....

And maybe, if he was lucky, she would let him put his hands on her, feel the pleasure of his mouth. Yes, maybe if he was lucky.

She brushed out her hair, coated her mouth in Scarlet Passion Red, and finally, when Mindy nodded with approval, Gillian was ready.

"You're sure," asked Mindy, perhaps noticing the dangerous gleam in Gillian's eyes.

"I'm positive," Gillian assured her, and then grabbed her purse, the one with the condom in its package hidden behind the picture of Princess Di, adorned in picture perfect wedding-day splendor. A girl had to have her dreams. As for the condom, that was her insurance policy, she told herself, eyeing the wayward girl in the mirror.

Just in case.

SMITTY'S WAS A Tin Cup institution. It was a hole-in-the-wall bar that had seen a good bit of line-dancing and table-dancing, all the more remarkable since Smitty's had no dance floor, only a clientele that didn't care. There was one main room with square tables for dominos, a pock-marked wooden bar, two pool tables in the back and an old barrel that was usually filled with crackers.

Ernestine Landry, the granddaughter of the original Smitty, paid the taxes on the place and poured the beer, but she wasn't a big fan of the name Ernestine and went by Landry instead, which was a holy word in the Texas football vernacular, usually spoken with awe and hushed tones of respect. On Thursday nights, Smitty's was always crowded, but tonight seemed especially packed, and Gillian didn't want to speculate on the cause, mainly because she knew she was the cause, and it would make her stomach queasy, and it was never a good idea to drink on a queasy stomach. It was an even worse idea to see a former nonlover on a queasy stomach, but she didn't want to dwell on that either, because it would only make her stomach troubles worse.

As Gillian made her way toward the bar, she refused to look around. She wasn't there to see anybody. She was there because it was hotter than Hades, it was Thursday night, and besides, Mindy would do the looking for her.

After Gillian was done not looking around, Landry approached, her gray-frizzled head reaching just above the wooden counter. "Tuesday night is ladies' night— tonight is Thursday. If you want half-price pitchers, you're out of luck."

"Lite beer for me and a Shirley Temple for Mindy," Gillian ordered, then she and Mindy seated themselves on two of the more stable stools.

Landry poked her head above the bar and stared pointedly at Mindy's belly. "People don't like pregnant women in bars. They come to a bar to practice sin without consequences. You are a walking consequence."

Mindy smoothed out the pink-checked ruffles over the swell, beaming angelically, because she was devilish that way. "You got a packed house tonight, and check out that tip jar, already full. If you don't want the pregnant lady, I will leave, but I'll take the evening's entertainment with me. You make the call."

"I don't like being referred to as the entertainment," protested Gillian.

In answer, Landry popped the cap off the bottle, and slammed it on the counter. Foam bubbled up, spilling over the sides, making a mess and wasting good beer. It was a clever ploy designed to increase sales, and once Landry's point was made, she stalked off to harass the next customer. Never one to waste good beer, Gillian drank while Mindy discreetly sipped at her drink, taking stock of familiar faces, the folks who had known her since birth. This was her home, and it had always hurt her that Austen had never been a part of it.

"He's here, isn't he?" Gillian asked. She could feel the eyes, and hear the whispers, but there was something more. A flutter of nerves and the pulse of a rabbit. Not a scared rabbit, but a frisky one.

"He's here," confirmed Mindy. "Eight o'clock, sitting alone, chair rocked back against the wall." She laid a twenty on the counter. "That's if you go talk to him."

Shocked, Gillian turned. "You think you need to pay me?"

"No. Brad bet you wouldn't have the guts. I knew better. If I win, I get to buy that new swirling footbath."

Normally, Gillian could not be bribed, coerced or blackmailed into doing something that she knew in her heart was wrong. In fact, those very strong ethical foundations were what made her good at her job. However, there was a heat sink burning at her back, a line of uneasy sensations walking down her spine. Austen had no idea what he did to her sanity and it was the main reason she was dying to get up and sashay across the room. Oh, how she wanted to deliver a stunning cut-down to Mr.

Hart, flash him her sexiest smile, then walk out, with every man eyeing the black spandex that hugged her butt in a strategic manner.

"I'll talk to him," Gillian announced, twisting in her seat to get a proper look and show the world she wasn't...

Holy smokes.

The man looked her over, the devil's own eyes lingering on her wardrobe choices and the curves underneath. Gillian squirmed, the barstool too small for a woman whose body was about to explode.

Maintaining a calm smile, she returned the look, and noticed the changes. His jeans no longer had holes in the knees. Unless she missed her fashion mark—which she never did—they were high-dollar ass-huggers, bleached just enough to look well-worn. The brown hair was still long, sexily tousled, the ends touched with a silvery gold, as if the angels had reached out and marked him as their own.

Sure, Austen Hart had returned in the standard class uniform of Tin Cup, Texas, but the trimmings were just a little off, a little telling. The button-downed shirt was more fitted, more "in." The boots more polished. The buckle on his belt shone like gold. A more clueless man might have been unaware of the differences, but not Austen. No, Austen would have made his sartorial choices on purpose, to make a statement, to remind the people of Tin Cup that Frank Hart's son did not exist anymore and this new and improved persona was there to dazzle and delight.

Sadly, Gillian thought she would be the only one to miss the old version.

Beer in hand, she walked toward him. Meeting his gaze, seeing that ready smile, she wondered if he knew how much she hated what he did to her. In her mind, she had rehearsed a thousand lines, but now, all she could think about was the sinful speculation in those unapologetic dark eyes. It used to be, she could almost catch his heart flashing in his eyes. Now they flashed with something else. Sex. Quickly, Gillian erased the naked Austen images from her brain.

Focus, girl.

As her feet carried her closer to the man, the bar lights rippled over him, spotlighting the comfortable set of his shoulders, the hard planes of his chest. It was a beautifully proportioned chest, more broad, more strong, more confident than she remembered. She kept moving, until she was so close that she could see the tiny lines of stubble on the jaw. Gillian stopped. Waited.

The silence in the bar grew ear-popping loud.

"Hey, Gillian," he said, his voice caressing her name, just as silky, just as sexy, just the same way he'd enthralled her in the past. Gillian smiled, a thousand watts of sexual promise. She was no longer the innocent lamb. Now she could fight the devil on his own terms—and win.

The grin he fired at her was lazy and warm, spreading through her blood like whiskey, blocking out painful memories she needed to keep. *Remember the white silky gown in the back of your closet,* she told herself. *Remember the tears, remember the taunts.* Ten years ago she would have succumbed to the grin, destined to repeat her past mistakes, but not any more.

Gillian leaned one hip against his table, lifted the bottle to her lips, and then took a languorous sip. Her eyes never left his, her lashes fluttering bedroom-low. With a steady hand, she held out the bottle in invitation.

"Want some?" Her voice was husky with nerves, but the sultry intent was pitch-perfect.

He nodded once. She raised the bottle higher, just out of his reach and her smile turned cold.

Slowly, deliberately, she poured Texas's best beer on the head of the easy-leaving Austen Hart. It was ten years too late, but damned if she didn't feel free.

Gillian lifted her head and sauntered out of the bar, the sound of his mocking laughter echoing behind her.

4

A GREAT EXIT ENTAILED finality. An actual leaving of the premises in order to seal the deal, but Gillian couldn't quite pull it off. Instead, she found herself in the graveled parking lot of Smitty's, digging through her purse in the meager light of the moon, "searching" for her keys, even though they were sitting right in plain sight. No, in truth, she was waiting for Austen *once again,* but at least this time he didn't disappoint.

Her eyes traced over him, searching for some hint of the boy she knew, but this man was a tall, dark stranger. The beer-dumping had only highlighted his charms. The thin cotton shirt clung to a powerful chest, his hair darkened to a weathered bronze. His smile was full of all that confidence he'd never had. Liquid dark eyes met hers without remorse, as if she were nothing but a floozy in a bar. Gillian could feel her rage building again. Anger at her own mistakes as well as his.

"Why did you show up here tonight?" she railed, kicking up gravel as she paced. "What did you expect?"

"Not the beer. Nice exit, though." He ran a hand through his hair and stared at her. *Ogled* would be the better word choice. The cherry-popping glance slid to the swell of her breasts, arrogantly resting there as if he knew what was underneath. He did.

That stopped her in her tracks. Gillian resisted the urge to cover herself, willing herself not to react. "I thought you had left," he continued, finally moving his eyes back to her face.

"Not me. I'm not the leaver. I'm not the one who has to run scared."

His brows rose. "Is that why you're waiting out here? Because you couldn't be the first one to leave? Stubborn, but unnecessary." She didn't like the taunt. That wasn't something he would have done in the past. He'd been thoughtless, but never cruel.

"I wasn't done yelling at you," she explained, which was mostly the truth.

"I didn't know you had started." The shrewd gaze was studying her, curious and aroused.

"Don't be cute," she snapped, not liking the fevered tension in the air, the way her anger felt too out of control.

"It's part of my charm." He leaned against a parked pickup, his hands in his pockets, a flagrant display of masculine swagger. It was another new trait; one that unnerved her. Gillian glanced down, quickly shifted her gaze from exactly where he wanted it to be.

Bastard.

This time, Gillian did cross her arms across her chest. The air was too hot, he was too hot, and she could feel the flames licking at her face, her skin and the budded tips of her breasts. "This was a mistake. I don't want to be here. I didn't want to put on a show for the entire town."

He shrugged easily, a smile playing around his mouth. "Could have fooled me."

"That was pride," she admitted, because pride was a better excuse than lust.

"If that was pride, then what is this?" he asked, seeming as if he knew the answer, seeming as if he expected her to fall in line, fall into his bed.

At that, Gillian told her body to get it together. She would not be played. Not by him. She released her arms from their candy-assed position, and rested against the judge's Honda. Languidly she crossed one long leg over the other, cocked her hips just so, because this was pride. This was ego.

This was war.

"You don't think I can resist you, do you?" she told him, her smile every bit as pulse-pounding as his. "You think I want to crack open your cookie jar? No, sir."

She saw a flicker in his eyes. "You didn't used to think that way."

"I got smart." Then she shrugged, a careless roll of one shoulder that brought his eyes back to her breasts, and brought the tingles back to her skin. "Did you leave because you were scared? Afraid you couldn't measure up?"

His warm smile froze. "You didn't used to be a bitch, Gillian."

"Back in the day, I was always a bitch. Knew it, did it, I owned it. But I wasn't mean to you. I was always good to you. Always careful, always kind. I wanted to make you a part of this town, and I didn't deserve to be left high and dry on the most important day of my life." She met his eyes squarely because this was more important than beer, more important than sex.

He flicked a hand impatiently. "It was a dance."

Did he think so little of her? There were others who might have, deservedly so. But not Austen. "I wasn't talking about prom." She didn't like the vulnerability in her voice, but she wanted him to know how much she hurt. "I gave my virginity to Sonny Emerson."

It should have been you.

For the first time, she saw a crack in the surface. The generous mouth twisted into one tight line. "Emerson's a moron."

"He was nice. He was handy. He was there."

Why weren't you?

This time, he was the one who looked away. "It wouldn't have worked out. You knew I wasn't in for the long haul. Hell, Gillian. It was only sex. It wasn't that big of a deal."

No big deal. Out of everything he had done, that was the killing blow. She was proud of the way she stayed so calm. The Austen she knew before would have never said those words. No, the boy she had trusted was gone. In fact, it made it that much easier to finally be the one to walk away. She grabbed her keys and gave him a tight smile. "I expected an apology. An explanation. Something more than 'not that big of a deal.' See ya."

She found her car, admittedly her heart a little more whole. The pride was wounded some, but a long ways from dead. Her fingers weren't even shaking when she put the key in the lock.

He put his hand on the car door, stopping her.

"I'm sorry."

Gillian told himself to get a grip, move on and drive away. The only problem with that was that she wasn't the coward here, he was. For ten years she had waited for those words, and they were sweeter than she could have imagined.

Why couldn't she stay away?

Her shoulders sagged in defeat, relief. Slowly she

turned, searching his eyes, telling herself that if he was toying with her, then by God, shooting him in the balls wasn't painful enough.

The arrogance had disappeared. In his face she could see the echoes of the past, a whisper of that aching need, unmasked for a second before he carefully hid it again. From inside the bar, music played, slow and sultry, people were laughing, having a good ol' time. But not Austen. Once again, alone and apart, and once again, the walls were up, and he pretended not to care.

"Are you sorry? Are you really?"

He took one step away from her, a tiny movement, but she saw. "I'm gone in the morning. I'm not coming back. You've got your apology. What else do you want from me?"

He sounded so angry at her, angry for wanting him, for trusting him. Ten years ago, she was foolish enough to do just that. Was she still?

No.

"I don't want anything from you. Not anymore. Tonight all I wanted was to embarrass you. Check. To make you hurt the way you hurt me, but that one is stupid, because I can't do that, can I? Goodbye, Austen Hart. Have an awesome life. I think I'll be the one to hit the road this time. It's late, and I have better things to do with my time. We're building a railroad through this town. Did you hear about that? Think on that one, Austen, because this town is moving on without you. We're hitting the big time, and you know who's going to lead that parade? Gillian Wanamaker. That's me."

She pushed his hand away.

"Gillian. Wait. Let's go to Peterson's Ride. Grab a six-pack. Watch the sky."

Oh, he was the clever one, all right. Throwing the

uncertainty in his voice, that same cautious trust that
had always lured her in the past. But he wasn't that boy.
She wasn't that girl.

The past was gone.

"Not the Ridge," she told him. The Ridge was a place
for innocent kisses and stolen dreams. Parson's Green
was much more basic. "Let's go to the Green."

Austen raised a brow. He no longer looked uncertain,
and she caught a glimpse of sadness in his eyes. "You're
sure?"

Her fingers tightened around the strap of her purse,
the condom tucked safely in its place.

This was an exorcism, a purging.

He'd been right earlier.

No big deal. This was only sex.

"YOU'VE CHANGED QUITE A BIT," Austen remarked,
handing her a longneck, brushing his fingers against
hers in what he hoped was a scalawag sort of way.

Gillian took the bottle of beer, leaned one elbow
against the old wooden steps and took a long, mouth-
watering drink. Her eyes were closed, no doubt appreciating the heady pleasure of icy beer on a steaming
night. Soon he was caught up in staring. Dazzled, just
like before, but when her eyes flickered open, his tough
expression was right back in place.

Along with extra weight in his shorts.

Parson's Green was to blame. The old ranch house
had been a whorehouse at one time, but after Lucky
Parson had died, it became the go-to spot for late-night
drinking, and summertime sex. Austen had spent some
nights here in his youth doing just that.

But never with Gillian Wanamaker.

"I've changed more than you know." Apparently

needing to prove this point, she flicked open two extra buttons on the black silk, treating him to a view that indicated that yes, her breasts had changed, too. Before, they'd been cute and perky. Now, they were round, full—man-sized. He tightened his man-sized fingers into a fist.

Gillian noticed.

"Are you trying to make me sweat on purpose?" It wasn't completely a joke.

"Are you?" She arched a brow, met his eyes. "Sweating? Boy, is it hot." She pressed the wet bottle against her throat, condensation glistening on her skin. Then she moved the bottle lower, and this time, condensation dampened her shirt. Twin peaks emerged and her smile was pure sin.

Holy hell, change was not good. Change was flat-out dangerous.

"I need to go." Austen scrambled to his feet, but the view from above was worse. She was every boy's dream. Her legs were golden in the moonlight, her lips juicy, her blue eyes knowing. She was every man's fantasy. His cock bobbed, happy to play its part.

"Running again?" Coolly she sat there, sipping her beer, as if this really was no big deal.

"This isn't you."

She cocked her head, shifted, her hips arching comfortably, or seductively, depending on a man's level of paranoia. "How do you know this isn't me?" argued the woman who was probably still a virgin. She'd probably lied earlier, or even more likely, he'd probably imagined the whole conversation.

Which was why he knew it was all a big lie. This woman wasn't real, only what he had always fantasized her to be. "Deep down the basic fundamentals stay true. Even yours." *Especially yours.*

Watching him with an impure eye, she flicked open another button, and he could see black lace, the devil's lace. A drop of sweat trickled down his neck. Courageously he carried on. "Sure there are some who have exceptional skills at concealing the fundamentals, but you can't turn yourself into something you're not."

Those knowing blue eyes studied him, admired him. "You've changed."

Instantly he seized on her mistake, the glaring flaw in her logic and some of the sex blood began flowing upstream to his brain. "I haven't changed a lick. I'm a little cleaner. I dress a little nicer, but no, I'm still the same." Just to prove it to her, just to see her jump, he bent down, and stroked an insolent forefinger over the hard bud of her nipple.

Gillian stayed perfectly still.

Uh-oh.

Realizing he was being outfoxed, Austen moved safely out of touching distance. "This isn't you," he repeated, to remind himself that Gillian Wanamaker was a pure and innocent soul, who did not participate in tawdry bedroom games.

Like a lioness rising to stalk her prey, she got to her feet and moved close, too close. She stroked a soft finger over his mouth, wetting her pouty lips, and he could feel his cock pushing up through his shorts.

"Maybe deep down, I was always a little bad."

Austen swallowed, not smart enough to step away. He could smell the faint bite of her perfume, the earthy aroma of beer, and the eau de female arousal. His cock throbbed even more. This wasn't Gillian. It couldn't be.

All he had to do was to show her who he was, and she would disappear.

Her smile turned slow and sure, but women had always underestimated Austen's ability to ruin a good thing. "Why are you doing this?" he drawled. "I didn't expect you to be so hard up. A girl like you. A body like that."

He saw her take the hit, saw the flinch on her face, and just like he wanted, the desire turned to fury. "Why? Why? Why did you leave that night? Why that one particular night? What was wrong with me?"

The plea in her voice was hard to resist, but he managed, flashing his cruel smile, the one he used when palms were waiting to be greased, the one he used when women started to look at him just slightly too starry-eyed. "You can't figure that one out? I'm a jackass, sugar. A first-class, blackhearted son of a bitch. I hurt people. I use people. It's what I do."

A sucker for punishment, she met his eyes and he wished he didn't see the conviction in hers. "I don't believe it."

He twisted a finger in her hair, brought their mouths inches apart. "Come closer and I can prove it. I'll strip you down, ride you hard, then leave without a second thought."

Still her stubborn gaze never strayed. "You think you can?"

"I know I can." His basic fundamentals were true. He was Frank Hart's son. The good part of him acknowledged that the good-for-nothing part was aching to taste her, to lock her beneath him, spread her legs and lose himself inside her.

Like a bad-girl wannabe, she pushed against his chest

and then took a step back, her body swaying to a silent rhythm, slow and sultry.

Hypnotized he watched, watched as she slid wicked fingertips over her breasts, watched as she pushed her hands through the silken strands of her hair, turning what had been a cute and pretty hair-do into the very best sort of bed-head.

It was a nightmare. It was a dream. Please, God, don't let him wake up.

Apparently someone was listening. Probably not God, because next, this woman locked her hands on to the porch post and twirled on her heels, not a move learned in cheerleader camp. It was a West Texas titty-bar twirl, and women like her were not supposed to be so well-versed in such antics.

His mind was drunk with the thought of it.

Letting go of the post, her hands strayed to her shirt, her curvy hips clocking back and forth in some primitive rhythm that he understood only too well.

Austen wanted to move, but as her hands worked the buttons, he stood frozen and stupid. In one irresponsible move, she stripped the shirt away, leaving nothing but a worthless piece of black lace that was a lot sexier than if she'd removed it.

His second instinct was to rip off his own shirt and cover her up. His first was to tear through the bra with his teeth. Usually Austen went with his gut, but this was Gillian.

Or it sure as hell looked like her.

Not done with him yet, she reached behind her back, twirled once, giving him a good bit of her back. It was safer, the simple stretch of her spine, the dusting of angel freckles. Just as his breathing resumed, she turned again, braless. His mistake—without the bra was a helluva lot sexier.

Sensing weakness in her prey, the woman looked at him with bedroom eyes, slowly licking her lips just once. His mind imagined that pink tongue wrapped around his cock.

Her smile grew.

Realizing that he was playing right into her sex-pot hands, Austen blinked, clearing the lusty fog from his vision. This was too important to screw up. She was too important to screw up. Lazily he leaned back against the opposite post, arms folded across his chest. He winked, an "aw-sugar" wink. It was condescending, sexist and insulting. It was masterful.

The smile faltered only a fraction. Then her blue eyes darkened to steel and those pretty fingers flirted with the side of her skirt. He dreaded the next move, even as every inch of him was panting to see it. The skirt slipped a paltry few inches, not lose enough to fall free.

Austen smiled.

She twirled on her heels, showing him her back. Novice, he thought.

Until she bent low from the waist, and eased the skirt down her legs, exposing a tiny black thong and a whole lot of temptation. Thankfully she was missing the heart attack on his face.

But by gawd, he would die a happy, happy man. Her ass—two perfectly sculpted mounds of muscle and sin. And this from a breast man. His cock tightened, ached, threatened humiliation. Still bent over, she grabbed the pole and rocked her delectable ass, hips swaying back and forth, and he could see her then riding him, just like he'd seen a thousand times in his mind. Unable to restrain himself, Austen moaned.

The woman heard.

With one graceful grind, she rose upright, hair tousled, lips moist and a body that begged to be ridden.

Strip her down, ride her hard.

The words were his, but the harsh voice in his head belonged to Frank Hart.

When she moved toward him, he didn't back away. Instead, he tweaked a rosy tip with an arrogant smile on his face.

She had no idea who he really was, what he'd seen, what he'd done, what he'd run from. Always running. There were hard lessons to be learned, but this woman needed to know, she needed to understand, she needed to forget.

When her hands shifted to his shirt, Austen stilled. Quick and efficient, she yanked the shirt from his shoulders. The tips of her nipples brushed against his bare skin like fire. Calmly he stood, cool and collected, in spite of the blood-pumping urge to touch.

Waiting, waiting.

Her hands moved to his fly, toying there, playing there, before sliding down the zip.

His cock leaped into her hand, a dog to its master, but this wasn't about sex anymore. This was about the fundamentals of his nature.

The waiting was done.

Callously he caught her hips in his hands and turned her to face the pole. He rubbed the slit between her legs, stroking the wet, swollen flesh. Her tail tilted higher. From the back, she was no different from any other piece of ass. Nothing more.

"No more playing, sugar," he said, shoving his jeans to his knees, sheathing his cock. He slid into her warm and willing passage, ignoring the pain in his head. This wasn't real, he told himself, only the fantasies of a thousand nights overlapping in his mind.

She rocked back against him, and he heard her pleasured gasp.

Strip her down, ride her hard.

His cock slid in and out, only the night watching two dogs at rutting season. She looked back at him, her face taught with confused pleasure. Austen closed his eyes and shoved harder, feeling her body buck under the overwhelming pressure. He would have broken under the pressure long ago. Not her.

She's not what you think. She's a tramp, a whore, and she's yours. All yours. They're all yours if you play the game.

"Is this…what you…wanted?" she managed, the words punctuated by the sharp slap of his thrust.

"It's what every man wants, sugar… Nothing else." His fingers gripped tighter on her hips, marking her skin, wishing she weren't so delicate. There'd never been bruises on her in his mind.

The ghosts of Parson's Green whispered around them, laughing like fools. Her back straightened, arching against him, pressing her skin to his sweat-soaked chest. His hips froze at the full-body contact, the clean silk of her hair caressing his face. For a second, he breathed in the virgin's scent of her, the essence of her. "Why did you leave?" she whispered. The words were loud in his head, breaking into his moment. She didn't need him, she was using him, just like he was using her, but the question hammered at him. He knew how to get rid of dreams. Destroy them.

Hell bent, he anchored her hips to his cock, pushed harder and harder, until she fell forward, her hands locking to the pole once again.

His eyes followed the desolate path of his cock, pumping deep inside her.

Over and over, he thrust. Relentless. Soulless. He could hear the sounds of her frantic gasps, felt the shudders course through her, and knew he had to remember this forever. He needed to finish this, finish her. Tension pulsed through her taut muscles, her body arching higher and higher, and he knew it was time.

With one vicious thrust, he spilled himself into the condom.

Her body froze, poised just on the edge, but he wouldn't give her that. He wouldn't give her the satisfaction she craved.

It was done.

Without a word, without a sound, he pulled out of her, ripped off the condom, not looking in her direction. Not now.

After she had cleaned up the mess that he'd made, he heard her laugh and Austen looked up. That was a huge mistake because the clear blue eyes were sparkling, not with humor, but tears. It was no less than he had expected, exactly what he intended. He wanted to pull her close, kiss every inch that he'd contaminated, but this was Gillian. She'd never needed his help. The blue eyes grew tougher, wiser and when she spoke her voice was cold.

"Take me back to the bar."

Austen curled up one side of his lip, just like his daddy used to do. "Sure thing, sugar."

Her eyes narrowed to hard slits and he reached out to pat her lightly on that magnificent ass. "If I had known what I was missing, I would have tapped this earlier."

She slapped his hand away, and jerked on her clothes. Once she glared in his direction, and he flashed her his most satisfied smile. She didn't look at him again. She didn't bother with her bra, wadding it into a ball, and chunking it at him with surprising force. The black slip of nothing fell at his feet. He picked it up slowly, held it out to her, but she shook her head. "For your collection."

He wanted to tell her he didn't have a collection, but she wouldn't have believed him. Instead, he stuffed the bra in his back pocket and politely took her arm.

"Watch your step. It's a little tricky. You don't want to fall and hurt yourself."

Not surprisingly, she turned, delivering a hard slap on his cheek.

Austen put his hand to his face, his fingers tracing there where she had touched him. The pain wasn't in his face, but somewhere far worse. Still, it had been the right thing to do. Hate and anger were so much healthier than all the fantasies he'd ever kept locked up inside.

Nonetheless, he frowned as he followed her to his car.

They drove in silence back to Smitty's where the parking lot was still full of cars. It had taken less than an hour to kill her dreams.

He walked around and opened her door, and she stared at him square on. In one swift movement, her feet hit the ground, and she pulled herself upright without his help.

The music from the bar filtered across the parking lot, along with the hum and buzz of the rest of the world. He was grateful for the masked silence, otherwise it'd be too easy to say things that he would regret.

He noticed the steel disappear from her eyes, watched the moonlight shimmer on her face, and he realized with a foolish heart that his dreams were still alive.

Not that it mattered. Tomorrow morning he would be gone, and Gillian Wanamaker would be nothing more than a movie reel in his head. Fantasy. Fantasy was safe.

"Don't pretend with me. You don't have to," she was saying, her eyes vacant yet smart. "Not anymore. I know who you are. Frank Hart would be right proud of his youngest boy. Living up to the family name."

Austen Hart nodded once, too tired to do anything else. She was right.

He watched as she wheeled around and walked toward her car, watched until her tail-lights disappeared into black.

It was over. It was done.

5

As GILLIAN QUIETLY unlocked her front door, her phone started vibrating.

Mindy.

No, not yet. "All fine. Talk in the a.m.," she texted back. It was a lie. Mindy would read it as such, but it would stall her friend until tomorrow.

When Gillian didn't feel so forlorn.

The door now open, she moved inside, careful not to disturb her—

Mother.

Modine Wanamaker was sitting on her favorite floral sofa, the one they'd moved in from the original Wanamaker home. Her knitting needles clicked away, until she spotted her daughter. Knitting aside, she was clearly waiting for her daughter to explain.

Damn.

"Hi, Momma." Gillian stored her purse in the bin in the front closet, lined up her shoes where they belonged. Ordinary sounded good. Routines were easy to follow, she didn't have to think.

Her mother watched her with solemn eyes. She didn't

have to see her mother to feel the look. That was the thing with families.

Gillian turned, tried to smile. "You shouldn't have stayed up."

"You're my daughter. You'll be my daughter until I die. If I think I should stay up, I will."

Gillian turned her attention from her mother to other less knowing objects like the antique glass collection perched on a ledge at the front window. She dusted the imaginary cobwebs. The collection was from the old house, too. One more thing that Gillian had insisted her parents keep. "You stayed up for nothing."

"I was worried. That's not nothing. Are you okay?"

Realizing there was no cobwebs, there would never be any cobwebs, Gillian faced her mother and forced a smile. "I'm peachy."

Her mother nodded once, then patted the cushion next to her. Obediently, Gillian sat.

"You are the best daughter a mother could ever have. You took us into your home without a second thought. Never complaining, not once. You work hard for yourself, for others, and especially for Emmett and I. And when you hurt, I hurt. When you ache, I ache. And those are things you can never hide, because I feel it here, just like you." Modine bumped a fist to her chest.

Her mother looked so tired, circles under her eyes, and Gillian felt so tired, as well. Drained. "I don't want to talk about this."

There were times when words were pointless, both Wanamaker women knew it. With a bone-deep sigh, her mother folded her into her arms. "I know. I was never a talker, either. He's one of the H-A-R-Ts, honey. He can't help the way he is. A cruel man for a father, and you read the rumors in the paper, a meth dealer for a brother and now Austen's up on indictment. Kickbacks. Graft. Corruption. Did you expect anything better? It's the way God made that family and I'm sure that He in His infinite wisdom had some purpose for that blight on humanity, but it always escaped me."

The tears started then. Gillian was a first-class cryer. Silent, dignified, it was the Wanamaker way. Her mother hugged her tighter, making little hushing noises that only made the tears run faster. Gillian could smell her mother's lavender fabric softener on her gown, the faint smell of vanilla, all mixed with the musky smell of sex.

Instantly, she pulled away, wanting to clean up, and her mother knew the signs, probably smelled the signs, as well. She let her daughter go, wiped away a few of the tears and held out a box of tissues for good measure.

"He'll be gone tomorrow and meanwhile you need to move on. Marry Jeff Junior. Have a good life, Gillian. You don't deserve the pain. Leave that to a stupid woman. That's not you."

Gillian blew her nose, dabbed her cheeks and studied the bluebonnet landscape on the wall. Serene and tough, very telling.

Done with the pain, she met her mother's eyes and nodded. "You're right, Momma. I don't deserve this."

Tomorrow he would be gone and Gillian wasn't going to cry over Austen Hart anymore.

AUSTEN SIGNED THE legal papers at 8:57 a.m. sharp. The lawyer, Hiram Handley, was the nice, kindly sort, not the blood-letting sort that roamed freely in the state capital.

"What are you going to do with your part of the property?"

Austen leaned back in the desk chair and laughed.

One-third of Hell House.

The house had originally been willed to Frank's brother Edward, who wisely escaped to California. Judging by the Christmas card that Austen received every year, Edward looked to be human. Or had been. Uncle Eddie had died six months ago, leaving the Hart land to the children of Frank Hart. Now Austen was back in Tin Cup, the proud owner of one-third of a stinking pile of shit.

What a prize.

And yet the lawyer was peering over his spectacles, expecting a serious answer. "Demolition, maybe."

He'd let Tyler handle that. Or, oh, no, can't forget Little Sis. No, the old house was somebody else's problem.

"Property's mineral rights will be worth something. Two miles east they ran a frac job and took a marginal site and the owner bought a condo in Aspen. With your connections, you should check into it."

No, he didn't want any money. Tyler didn't need any money, but his sister, Brooke? His stomach clenched. He wanted to keep Brooke as far away from here as possible.

"One more thing. Tyler mentioned something about Frank and Charlene having another kid. A girl. Do you know how to contact her?"

Austen shook his head. "Check with Tyler."

He'd be gone even if she did show up to claim her share. Did it matter if she knew he'd lied to her about the upstanding Harts of Tin Cup, Texas? Nah. As long as he wasn't here to face it.

Relieved to be done, he vacated the chair and charged for the door.

"If you need anything," the lawyer called, "you have my number…"

Austen was already gone.

Outside, his Mustang was waiting for him. Shelby was what he called her, and she was his pride and joy. The closest thing to a relationship he'd ever had. A 1968 fastback, rebuilt with all the original parts, including a 428 Cobra Jet V8 engine, Holley carbs, and cherry-red with white racing stripes down a scooped hood. Austen climbed in, heard the steady rumble of the engine and headed for home.

Home. Away from all the ghosts, away from all the rumors and lies. Away from here. Coward, that he was. Just like his daddy.

Hell.

Austen had spent his life running from a ghost. Maybe this time, he should kill the ghost for good.

There were two routes to the highway and Austen made himself take the shorter one, Pecos to Chestnut Drive to Elm, down the long dirt road to the old house two miles off Orchard Street.

He eased his car to a stop, but didn't get out. This was close enough.

There was only one house on this road. An empty dirt field on either side, nothing for miles around but Hart property. No one had ever wanted to be near them. The morning was so quiet, birds singing, the wind whistling in the trees and somewhere in the distance he could hear a shotgun blast and a raspy laugh. Fun times.

After taking a deep breath, he took a more objective look. Without anyone to care for the house, the paint was nearly gone. The front porch was slanting precariously to one side, and there seemed to be a bird's nest under the eaves. At least somebody could be happy there.

In the harsh light of day, it wasn't imposing or scary. It was only sad.

Exactly like Frank Hart, the man. In the harsh light of day, he wasn't scary or imposing either, only sad.

And now Austen was here, kicking the ass of a long-festering wound, the proud owner of one-third of nothing.

Hasta la vista, baby, he said to himself and pulled away from the curb. He drove down Main, by the courthouse, not really scanning for anyone in particular. Sightseeing, that was all. He passed Zeke's garage not bothering to stop. Austen had left his old employer under questionable circumstances. Over time he'd paid back the six hundred—anonymously, since regret only went so far.

His foot pressed a little harder on Shelby's accelerator. Feeling the kick in the engine and Austen was happy to see the dump in the rearview mirror.

He drove past Live Oak, past the Wanamaker house, and slowed to a conservative five miles per hour in case any kids happened to be around.

There were no kids on the tree-lined street, no early morning gardeners, no Gillian at all. He told himself that it was for the best. When the street curved, the house disappeared and he headed for the freeway, free and clear, until his cell phone rang.

Austen pulled to the shoulder and took the call.

"On your way home, darling?"

It was Carolyn. Austen latched on to the familiar voice, feeling normalcy return.

"Leaving now."

"I have a surprise for you when you get here."

At the sound of her husky laugh he frowned, not thrilled with the idea of sex just then. In fact, celibacy seemed like a great plan. Unfortunately, barring below-the-waist paralysis, he wasn't sure that Carolyn would believe a so-called lifestyle change. Maybe he could tell her he was gay? Nah. That wouldn't go over well, either.

"Don't you want to know about the surprise?"

No. "Sure."

"I was having dinner with Jack Haywood last night, and you know he's tight with the transportation committee and all, and he was unhappy with the proposed rail route. So we moved it."

Austen punched the record button on his phone. Some conversations needed to be listened to twice. "We moved it? Carolyn, you can't just reroute a plan that's been on the books."

"Not me, exactly. Mainly some of the oil lobby. And Pecos County. Seeing as the price of a barrel is shooting back up, Jack figures that shifting everything forty miles east will revitalize all those little towns that don't have oil revenues to sustain their growth in the long term."

That, and Jack Haywood grew up in Boxwood Flats, one of those little towns that was forty miles due east. Austen rubbed the throbbing ache at his temples.

"Your dad's okay with all this?" Austen knew the governor would put his foot down. The governor would stop it.

"He was more than happy after the Pecos county rep said he'd vote yes on Dad's new budget. He's been grinding his teeth to get that thing passed before the election."

Hell. "Jack's been a busy guy."

"I thought it was brilliant, killing like fifteen birds with one stone. I know you're not fond of Tin Cup.

Yes, sir, if I had a nickel for every time you wished a hurricane on that town."

Austen closed his eyes. "There are no hurricanes in West Texas. It was a metaphorical hurricane."

"You say metaphorical. I say they don't need a rail station. I thought you'd be happy."

Gillian was going to be furious. He remembered the pride in her voice. *We're building a railroad through this town. We're hitting the big time.*

Hell.

Gillian would think he was responsible. Austen Hart, lowdown, sexist, town-killing, parade-killing jackass of the year.

She would hate him.

She already did.

"I am happy," he lied. "Has the story hit the wires?" It was a tiny story. Metro only. Probably page seventeen of a Sunday late edition. Nobody would notice.

"Some of the local outlets picked it up, but Daddy's planning a formal press conference next week. He's calling it The NAFTA Pipeline: Bringing Jobs to Texas, The Big Engine that Could. The slogan was my idea."

"When's the press conference?"

"Monday. First thing."

Monday. He felt immediate relief and let out a long breath. That was three days away. A lifetime. He'd be in Austin. Hell, she probably would have forgotten his name by Monday.

After he told Carolyn goodbye, he pulled back on the highway and cranked up the volume on the radio.

There was nothing he could do. *Do not care. Not my problem. Not my fault.*

On the radio, some male singer was crooning about

the woman he loved, the one who was not his wife. About the guilt weighing like bricks on his heart.

Austen flipped stations.

This time, it was the female whining about the cheating bastard she loved, and how she hoped he would be barbecued in hell.

Damn country and western.

Now frustrated and guilt-ridden, Austen shut the radio off. He was the jackass of all jackasses. He deserved the guilt. And yet, would he turn around and solve the mess he'd just heard about? Not in a million years.

Traffic was starting to pick up on the highway, and he could hear an emergency siren coming from behind.

There was nothing in the mirror, but the sound was getting louder. He checked again and this time he could see the flashing red lights approaching over the hill.

He checked the speedometer just in case. A law-abiding seventy-five miles per hour. Not a problem.

The red lights pulled closer, and he shifted to the next lane so the cop could pass.

The headlights of the car began to flash in his mirror, and right then he knew. Peaceful acceptance filled his mind, a trick that he'd learned as a kid. Anticipation was always the worst.

His first instinct was to pull over, let her rant and then drive off without a care. But for once, he was innocent. Better to run. He didn't need the harassment. He didn't want to see her again.

He wasn't that strong.

Figuring she'd eventually give up, he cruised along at his little-old-lady speed.

Gillian was smart.

In the rearview mirror, he could see her bright lights growing brighter, trails of white oil-burning steam spilling from under her hood. Somebody was going to be in trouble, and this time it wouldn't be him. He started to point toward her hood, but then she sped on past him. Her brakes screeched, assaulting his ears like a cat in its death-throes. The sheriff's cruiser stopped sideways in front of him, and he could hear the pained sound of rotors grinding through to the steel.

Hell.

Austen slammed on his brakes, no screeching, no squealing, no grinding, and the tires bit into the pavement. The smell of burned rubber assaulted his nose.

Hell.

At last, his Mustang stood still, and she was very lucky that he'd avoided a crash.

Furious, Austen jumped out of the car, watching as Dirty Harriet stalked toward him, complete with skintight jeans, dark sunglasses and one hand to her gun.

Good God, the woman was smoking—as was her car.

"What the hell did you do?" she yelled, whipping off her glasses and he could see the hurt in her eyes.

"I had nothing to do with it."

"Bull shit."

Austen knew this was going nowhere. He had excellent situational evaluation skills. Opting for retreat, he opened his car door and slid behind the wheel. For good measure, he slammed the door. Hard. Wincing at the sound because Shelby had sensitive doors.

"You're not leaving until this is fixed. You're not leaving until you tell me exactly what you did," she warned.

Be the jackass. Embrace the jackass. Austen shifted the Mustang into Reverse. "Watch me."

She pulled out her Glock and aimed it at his left front tire. Her smile was pure evil.

Scorching heat filled the car, or maybe that was just her fury. "Dammit, Gillian."

Gillian blew on the black polished barrel. "I'm a good shot, Austen. Don't tempt me."

Austen considered driving away, but he could see the determination in her eyes. That, and his death. That, his death and the smell of leaking antifreeze that indicated her car wasn't going anywhere.

No, Austen didn't have the will to fight her. Not now, not over this. Not when he deserved it. This Gillian—the pissed off, deadly Gillian—was safe.

Resigned, he turned off the engine, but was smart enough not to leave the safety of the vehicle. "I didn't do it."

"Then why are they changing the train route now?"

"It's Jack Haywood and Carolyn."

Gillian put her hands on her hips. "Carolyn, the governor's daughter. The one you're banging. That Carolyn? Why does she bother her pretty bobble-head with Tin Cup, Texas, population two-thousand, one hundred and forty-seven, a mere speck of flotsam on the political landscape of this fine state?"

Why couldn't she be stupid? Austen sighed. "She did it because she thought it would make me happy."

To be completely fair, Gillian absorbed that fact better than he thought she would. Her face grew calm, nearly peaceful. The angry haze cleared from her eyes and she holstered her weapon.

Austen managed a smile.

Wearing an angelic smile herself, she leaned into the driver's-side window and it was hell all over again.

Her sunflower-yellow hair brushed his arm, her 'Not in This Lifetime' perfume teased his nose, and all he could remember was last night's mouthwatering striptease and the mind-blowing joy of being inside her. Quickly he refocused on the other Gillian. The clothed, uniformed, armed Gillian.

"You're going to fix this," she was telling him. "We're going to make a plan, and you will fix this."

In spite of his best intentions, his mind was still locked on the imagery of her bare ass in his hands, so her words didn't compute for an embarrassing few seconds.

Then, he realized what she was insisting. How she was going to drag him into this massive political mess. No way. No how.

"This is not my problem."

Her eyes grew fierce.

"Do not give me that, Austen Hart. I have let you con me, I have let you screw me, but that was us. This is bigger than that. This is our home. This is our community. This is our town."

"Your town. Never mine."

Her eyes softened infinitesimally. "He's dead."

Words, nothing more. Austen made his living from words, and he knew that words didn't do shit. "I. Don't. Care."

Then, because she was always the one who could twist him best, Gillian leaned closer, close enough that he could read everything in those sky-blue eyes. The hurt, the pain, but it was the faith in him that was like a dagger to his chest.

"Do it for me," she pleaded.

If she had still been mad, he could have said no. If she had been the temptress, he could have driven away.

But no. Not this. "I'm not making any promises," he said, needing her to know he was going to disappoint her. Getting that right out in the open.

"I'm not asking for any promises," said the girl who expected the moon.

"It's not going to work. When Jack Haywood was born, he came out with a hand on the doc's wallet, and a direct line to the governor's mansion. Sometimes his taste in women is a little questionable, but by and large, the man's a political miracle worker."

"You could work miracles if you wanted to." She used her cheerleader's voice, the one when the team had been down by six touchdowns. The same cheery confidence that made the quarterback throw a little farther, made the fullback run a little harder. In the end, everybody still lost because nobody came back from six touchdowns. Ever.

In Austen's not so humble opinion, miracles didn't happy in Tin Cup, Texas, and they sure as hell didn't happen to men like him. They didn't even happen to Gillian Wanamaker, no matter how badly she wanted to believe.

On the other hand, Austen was older, wiser, and he knew how to play the game. He knew how to smile with all the confidence of the world's greatest snake-oil salesman. And Gillian smiled at him in return, buying it hook, line and sinker.

"You want a miracle? You got it," he said, but there was a twinge in his chest that was fast becoming a pain in the ass. He prayed to God that he wasn't growing a conscience because it was twenty-eight years too late.

6

THERE WAS AN OMINOUS hissing sound coming from under the hood, and the engine light was solid red. Car problems? Now? Really?

It wasn't fair.

From his spiffy, happily running Mustang, Gillian could see the smile on Austen's face. As if a mere woman was too "fragile" to understand the workings of an engine.

Ha.

Shooting a capable glare in his direction, she shut down the engine, and went to take a look. Competently she opened the hood and immediately spotted the problem. Steam was billowing from the round cap on the big tank. Obviously the tank wasn't happy. Possibly she should have taken the car in when the warning light had flashed, but she'd been busy, and the light had gone off. It had definitely gone off.

She swiped at a mosquito, snuck a look at Austen who was still sitting comfortably in his own reliable transport. There were three choices: call for help from the station, ask Austen for help or figure this out herself.

How hard could it be?

Remove the cap, relieve the pressure…

"Don't touch the cap," Austen warned, appearing next to her, grease rag in hand.

Gillian rolled her eyes. "Do I look stupid?"

He bent over the car and used the rag to twist the cap, his cotton T-shirt clinging to his nicely formed back, not that she was noticing or anything. "You're leaking anti-freeze. Hose is busted. And you most likely ground out your brakes with that last stop."

"Oh," she contributed intelligently. "You think the car will make it back to town?"

His eyes were amused, dammit. "Like this? No."

"Oh."

"Give me a second," he said, and strolled over to his Mustang, buried his head in the trunk.

"If you think that just because I'm letting you fix my car, that I'm also letting you off the hook, then you've got another thing coming."

The man didn't even look intimidated, strolling back with a battered toolbox in hand. Ungraciously, he dropped it at her feet. "Nope." While she quietly steamed, he pulled out a run of black rubber hose, and sliced off a section.

Next he replaced the length of hose in her car, twisting, tightening, with nary a word of complaint.

Ten minutes later, the hose was replaced, the radiator was filled with water and he wiped his hands on the rag, staring at her expectantly.

"Don't think I'm going to thank you for that. I knew what to do."

He cast a long look at the highway, and she knew if he took off again, this time she wouldn't stop him.

Instead, he looked at her. "Let's get back to town."

"You're coming with me?" she asked, sounding hope-ful, wishing she didn't.

"That car is a death wish on wheels. As a man with a conscience, I don't have a choice."

ONCE AGAIN IN THE claustrophobic confines of Tin Cup, Austen insisted that Gillian park the sheriff's cruiser in the town lot, and exchange it for another vehicle, which he personally inspected before she followed up on an overturned feed truck. While he waited, he checked out the mistreated cruiser, making a mental list of the work that needed to be done. The oil was calcified sludge. The belt was worn to threads, and the front brake pads needed to be replaced.

Not that he was going to do anything about it. He went back to waiting in the air-conditioned comfort of her office, making a list of exactly what parts and work she would need, not that Zeke would try and pull a fast one on the sheriff, but Austen thought he should cover all the bases—just in case Zeke had been corrupted.

After that, he pulled out his phone, sat in her chair and began making calls. He left four messages for Jack and explained to Maggie Patterson that he wasn't sure he would make Saturday night's charity dinner.

"But it's your project," Maggie cried. "Why don't you ever go? I know Ed's not working you that hard."

"Now, Maggie. You ever seen me dressed up in some monkey suit? Not my style." As he talked, he frowned at the grease underneath his fingernails and realized he needed to wash his hands before Gillian returned.

"It would mean a lot to Ed," she was saying. "It would mean a lot to me. It would mean a lot to those boys. You could be a role model for them." Much like her husband, Maggie would say whatever needed to be said in order to get things done her way. Austen had worked as a lobbyist for Big Ed Patterson's firm for nine years, and he knew better than most.

"No, ma'am."

Maggie's sigh was heavy with disappointment, but Austen wasn't about to dress up like some shining model of moral virtue. Hell.

After that, he got one text message from Tyler, asking how things were, and Austen scanned the confines of the Tin Cup sheriff's office, and quickly typed out a reply: "Having a great time. Wish you were here."

Seeing as Tyler had always believed Austen's line of hooey that Austen was Tin Cup's favorite son, the sarcasm would be lost, which always cracked Austen up. Such was the complicated nature of their brotherly relationship. Austen had never believed that people truly wanted to hear the truth. Tyler didn't understand why people needed to lie. Whatever worked.

Austen tilted back in the chair, felt the loose screw and shook his head at the slapdash way the town was falling apart around him. It took a few minutes of digging to find a screwdriver, but eventually he spied one buried in the metal supply cabinet—with hinges that needed to be oiled. Ten seconds later, the chair was rocking and rolling like God had intended and the metal supply cabinet no longer squeaked.

The clock was ticking on the wall. It was nearly noon, and still no word from Gillian. He stared at his list of repairs, paused, then made up his mind.

Hopefully Zeke still kept the shotgun unloaded. If not, well, Gillian would have to find some other sap to fix her problems. Did he look like Don freaking Quixote?

Not even close. Frankly, he should just call it a day, hop in the Mustang and leave the town eating his dust.

He didn't.

Instead, he strolled down to Zeke's old garage, as if he were the favored son. The front door was open, like it always was, and Austen hesitated. The radio was blasting old George Jones, exactly like it always was. He should go inside.

He glanced across the street where the abused sheriff's car was parked in the lot. In his heart, Austen knew it was inhuman to walk away from a vehicle in such poor shape, so he made his feet move and went inside his place of old employ.

Zeke was in the only bay, hunched over a tire, wearing the usual blue coveralls.

"Hey, Zeke," Austen called out in greeting, checking the garage for the shotgun, breathing a sigh of relief that the shotgun was gone.

Slowly the old man untwisted himself. His faded grey eyes were a little puffier than the last time Austen had seen him, and a lot less friendly. "Don't need you here."

It was nothing more than he deserved, but Austen managed a grin. "I need to buy some parts from you." He pulled out his wallet. "I got cash."

Zeke shifted his feet with a creak of bones and spit on the ground. "I don't take funny money."

Austen stopped smiling, because it was getting too hard to fake. "Gillian's car is a wreck. She's going to be out on the highway, tearing after some trucker who's texting while he drives, and her engine's going to blow, or the brakes are going to give, and then where will y'all be? All I need is a set of pads, antifreeze, an alternator belt and some oil. Charge me five times market if it makes you feel better, but don't hurt her."

Zeke pulled out his rag, wiped his hands and sighed. "I suppose it won't hurt."

"I'm sorry," Austen told him, not that he wouldn't do it all over again, but he'd never meant to betray the old man's trust.

Zeke met his eyes, more forgiving than before. "I would have loaned you the money."

"I know. I couldn't ask."

The man nodded once, signaling an end to the conversation. "All right. Tell me what you need."

IT WAS AFTER FIVE O'CLOCK by the time Gillian dragged herself into the office, the uniform sticking in unfortunate places, and her hair sadly flat. When she walked in, Austen sat at her desk, hair still shower-damp, clothes freshly pressed, marvelously studly looking, and she wanted to cry.

Immediately he got up from the chair, and Gillian collapsed into it, frowning at the unusual lack of flexibility.

"Long day?" he asked in a concerned voice.

"It's not over yet."

"Tell me what to do. I can help."

"You mean that?" she asked, spinning once, noticing the lack of squeaks. Austen watched her with nonchalant eyes.

"Don't read anything into it. It's better than sitting around on my ass. Besides, this way I get to leer at yours." He wiggled his brows, and she sighed because he made it very difficult to hate him, no matter how hard she needed to.

She spun around in her chair again, waiting for the

ancient noises, but there were none. Curious, she poked
her head underneath, wondering if someone had slipped
in a new chair while she wasn't looking, but it looked
the same. Then she looked at Austen, a question in her
eyes, but he was all "not going to say a word" and even
though she had her suspicions, she chose to keep them
to herself. After that, she dragged him downstairs to
the jail where he proved quite helpful by convincing
the town librarian, Martha Connelly, to drop larceny
charges against Bo Brown, who had turned in a library
book seventy-two days late.

When she was on the phone explaining to Mayor
Parson that yes, she had heard about the revised train
route, and yes, she had a bulletproof plan to get the
station back, Austen had the presence of mind not to
laugh.

He helped her pack up seven chocolate cream pies for
the rummage sale, and unlike Mindy, Austen expressed
great admiration for the mile-high meringues.

For a man who had only last night been the very
picture of poor manners, today, he had moments of
heart-touching thoughtfulness, and possible chair-fixing
skills.

Austen Hart was one of those long-forgotten puzzles
with a few missing pieces hidden under the couch.

At the rummage sale prep, her mother smiled politely
at him, and then promptly took Gillian out into the back
half of the church.

"Do you know what you're doing?"

"Have you heard about the new route," Gillian re-
plied, keeping her voice discreetly low. "The Trans-
Texas route, the one that is *not* passing through Tin
Cup?"

Her mother's mouth quivered in horror, both at the

awful news, and also the realization that the town grape-vine was running slow. "Is he responsible?"

"How could that be? He was here, Momma," Gillian patiently explained, even though yes, he was partially responsible. However, in the eyes of both Gillian and the law, it didn't warrant a full indictment of guilt.

"Then why is he still in town? Is this some wild hair of yours?" her mother asked, as if Gillian had wild hairs every day of the week.

"He's going to help us. He's going to get the route back to the way it was."

Her mother shook her head. "He's going to make you cry again, that's what he's going to do."

"Impossible. All I need is a couple of hours to see what's the best plan of action, and then I send him on his way." She smiled at her mother, an indication of confidence in both her superior problem-solving skills, and also Austen's miracle-working capabilities, each highly overrated in Gillian's mind, but the ability to achieve greatness usually started as a mental condition.

"You aren't going with him to Austin, are you? What about Mindy? Did you forget about the shower? The talk with Mindy?"

Gillian shook her head. "Momma, Momma, Momma. You think I'd skip out on my best friend and my respon-sibilities here to go gallivanting around the state with some man in a hot car?"

"Only that man," her mother muttered, folding her arms across her chest.

Gillian wrapped her mother in a quick hug. "Don't worry about me. I'm too busy to be gallivanting any-where." Right then her cell rang and Gillian waved at her mother and left.

AUSTEN HART WAS NOT the miracle worker she believed. For two hours they argued in his room at the Spotlight Inn, and they were no closer to finding a way to switch the rail route back to its original route via Tin Cup. The man had the power of negative thinking down to a fine art.

"You don't know politics, Gillian. Your elected officials sell their souls on a daily basis. Haywood took some of the most ornery players in the state economy—the developers, the oil industry and the East Texas legislators—and put them in bed together. Speaking from a purely analytical perspective, it's brilliant. I'm shocked I didn't think of it myself."

He was sprawled in a chair, mainlining coffee, and there was a deviant gleam in his eyes.

"Those are the bad guys, Austen. We're not supposed to admire them."

"Occupational hazard," he told her, looking unabashed and unashamed. It wasn't normal for Gillian to be this drawn to a morally flexible personality. After high school, she had stuck to the straight and narrow—mostly. So why this twitchy itch to launch herself at him? Her gaze lingered on the long, lean body, the powerful thighs, the deep dark eyes. And then there was the denim-covered screaming rocket that bulged beneath his fly.

Oh, yeah. Money wasn't the root of all evil. It was the penis.

Specifically the penis of Austen Hart. The thick, lively, jack-hammering penis of...

Gillian grabbed the complimentary bottled water and chugged. Then she tapped her pen on the empty sheet of paper. "Can we go back to the governor?" she asked. "Obviously, he liked the original plan."

Austen considered that. "We could try it. He's going down in the polls, the budget is in trouble, the oil market isn't roaring back as fast as the industry thinks it should and it's an election year. Absolutely the perfect time to have the public think that he'll turn on a dime."

Gillian was not dissuaded. "What could sway him back?"

At her innocent question, he laughed. "Nothing, unless he died."

She liked watching Austen think when he thought nobody was watching him. His face was animated and open. Lovable.

They tossed around a few more useless ideas until finally Gillian gathered her courage to bring up the one that kept beating at her brain. "What about the daughter? Carolyn? I mean, she's the one who made this mess. Can you persuade her to unmake it?"

Austen was visibly shocked. "There are things that I'll do, but that's not one of them."

So now he's got sexual ethics? Still, his answer pleased her. "Something's changed?"

"No," he said coldly and it was like watching the Berlin Wall come up.

"Then why?" she pressed.

Austen remained stubbornly silent, his eyes fixed somewhere beyond her. Eventually he stood and picked up the flyers. His brows drew together in a confused frown. "Haywood had to promise something to Big Ed and he did it without me knowing, which is no easy feat."

"Big Ed?"

"Ed Patterson. He runs the association of oil and gas producers and he's my boss. He doesn't have a change of heart unless he's getting something out of it. There was a sweet deal in place for him when the route was negotiated."

Gillian followed his line of thinking. "Somebody promised him something more?"

He shot her a sideways glance. "Nothing that would make the papers."

"Is this what the indictment's about?"

Austen frowned. "What indictment?"

"Kickbacks, bribery, graft, corruption," she told him, dancing around his situation, and hopefully he'd help her out.

"The governor?" he asked, not helping her out at all.

Gillian hesitated before finally blurting out the truth. "You."

He squinted hard, and then paused before answering. "I'm not worried. You shouldn't be either."

"It's nothing?" she asked cautiously.

He waved a hand. "Part of doing business, that's all."

Relieved at his answer, Gillian pretended she wasn't worried. He was right, people got brought up on indictments all the time. All the same, she didn't want him in trouble. In spite of all the ways that he'd hurt her, she didn't want to see him hurt. She told herself that such thinking was the result of her charitable upbringing, that he shouldn't be held responsible for bad acts because he'd been raised by the world's most obnoxious drunk. She told herself that her heart was unmoved and untouched, but she worried she was wrong.

However, there were more immediate problems to worry about. The train route, for example. "So was the governor's new deal illegal? We find out, expose it and we'll have trains in Tin Cup once again."

Austen laughed, which he shouldn't have, since it was a darned good notion, and shouldn't it be treated as such? "Only in the movies, Gillian. They didn't break any laws. They did something worse. They did things that look bad politically and in an election year nobody likes when the spotlight hits the backroom where the deals are made. People get very, very angry. See, what you do is find out and then merely *threaten* to expose it. Friendly persuasion."

"Extortion," she said flatly, disturbed by the immoral direction of the conversation. Disturbed that parts of her liked it. Or maybe it was the excitement in his eyes, the way she could feel the hum in her parts. Gillian had always been drawn to wicked things, but usually she was able to resist. At that thought, she frowned, and crossed her legs more firmly together.

"All we have to do is find out—" he started, and was interrupted by a banging on the door.

"Gillian!"

Austen looked at her. "Who the hell is that?"

"Jeffrey."

"Jeff Junior?" Austen sounded incredulous rather than jealous.

"He's very successful now," she defended, raising her voice to be heard above Jeffrey's pounding.

"Gillian! Are you all right?"

Austen made no move to answer the door. In fact, he appeared completely unconcerned. "Well?" she asked, miffed by his lack of concern.

"He's after you, not me."

"But it's your room. You should answer it. I'm only a guest."

Finally noticing her discomfort, Austen began to smile. "He suspects we're doing something?"

"Open the door," she demanded, because the roguish look on his face was starting to alarm her.

Without warning he reached for her, pulled her tight in his arms and kissed her.

Retribution had begun, wicked retribution.

Sweet retribution, she thought, getting dizzy from the feel of his lips. Her hands crept into his hair, locking him tighter, deepening the play of her tongue.

Who needed the straight and narrow when they had this?

His hands slid underneath her shirt, marauding over her skin and her breasts, the banging on the door an unnecessary distraction.

Long, earth-shattering moments later, Austen pulled back and brushed a careless thumb over her swollen mouth. "Now you look like we're doing something." He acted like the whole thing was nothing more than a ploy. If it hadn't been for the backlit flames in his eyes or the uneven breathing, she probably would have been ticked, but Mr. I Feel Nothing had a hard-on bigger than Texas.

Her sexually conflicted self heaved a sigh.

"Gillian!"

Now back in the present, Gillian jerked open the door, ready to calmly explain to Jeffrey that theirs was an uncommitted relationship and she didn't need another babysitter.

His innocent eyes were wide, shocked. "For crying out loud, Gillian, button up when you answer the door."

What?

Her gaze flew to her unbuttoned blouse, the daisy-covered bra riding a little lower than what the manufacturer had intended. Realizing that she'd been played, she whirled around, repairing her clothes, noticing the satisfied smirk on Austen's face.

Bastard, she mouthed silently.

He raised his brows and shrugged.

Once her clothes were restored to their proper place, Gillian turned back to Junior…*Jeffrey.*

"Why are you here?"

"We were supposed to meet for dinner," stated the man who had never lied in his life.

"We were not."

His face flushed with embarrassment. "Well, not exactly, but…" He trailed off, searching for his words. Eventually he found them. "I was worried. People were talking abut what happened last night."

Gillian glanced at Austen because he was to blame, except for the part where she went all out to seduce him, and then he got all jerky, and she got all teary, and all she wanted was to seduce him all over again.

Austen's expression was carefully blank.

Then Gillian looked at Junior, who was good-hearted and faithful and didn't inspire her to seductive thoughts at all. "Exactly what were they saying, Jeffrey?" she asked, her voice magnificently angry, because she was. At herself.

"They said you dumped beer on him. That you were furious at him."

"She's not so furious now," Austen interjected, choosing this moment to interrupt what should have been a private conversation.

Gillian glared at him over her shoulder, eyes promising slow death. "You'd be surprised at how furious I am now."

Jeff, gentleman to the end, held out his arm. "Let's go, Gilly."

She was tempted. Unfortunately, Jeff wasn't the cause of said temptation. "Don't look like that," she snapped, seeing how pleased Austen was. There was only one Master Manipulator in this town, and it was her.

Though right now, there was still work to be done, and somebody had to do it. She waved a tired hand in Junior's direction. "Go home, Jeff. I'm fine. I'm touched by your concern for my—"

"—ass," interrupted Austen.

"—well-being," she continued through her locked jaw, "but I don't need it."

"Gillian," Austen said from behind her.

"Can I finish?" she said, not looking at him, because he might not care about the people of this town, but she did.

Then Austen handed her the radio, turning up the volume, and she heard the dispatch, "10-54. We got a passle of goats grazing out on FM 1432. All units, and bring the cattle prods. Dogs if you got 'em."

"It's for you," Austen explained.

Emergency trumped all. Gillian grabbed her keys and slung her bag over her shoulder. "I'll be back later," she said to Austen, meeting his eyes. "Don't do anything to disappoint me."

After that, she turned to go, missing the worry on his face.

7

THREE HOURS AND one goat rodeo later, it was long past supper, and Gillian was sitting at her kitchen table, pricing rummage sale items and planning a baby shower. These were the normal Tin Cup days, but her mind was racing forward to Austen's upcoming task, i.e. fixing the rail route.

"Mindy, do you think I'm too confident?" asked Gillian while trying to decide if a cross-stitched flower pillow was worth twenty-five cents or one dollar. Certainly the smart price was twenty-five cents, but Gillian didn't want people to think her family had cheap things, so she wrote one dollar on the tag.

"Absolutely."

"Do you think I'm too certain that I can do whatever I put my mind to, no matter if it's impossible or not?"

"Without a doubt," answered Mindy, scratching over the one dollar and repricing it to a quarter.

"Speaking truthfully, have I ever so screwed up that you thought, 'That poor Gilly, she's losing it.'"

"Only once."

Gillian turned her attention to the last item on the table, a blue cashmere sweater adorned with seed pearls.

It was a timeless classic and worth something. Worth a lot. In fact, thirty dollars sounded like a bargain, high enough to know it wasn't cheap, and low enough to make the customer think it was a steal. Boldly she inked in thirty. "Am I losing it?"

"I'm guessing that you lost it again last night and are just now feeling the hard ground hit you in the butt."

Gillian looked at her best friend, knowing Mindy would listen to her forever and never complain, or switch the subject, or stifle a yawn. No, Mindy was the best, and as such, deserved for Gillian to shut up.

"I invited you here to discuss the plans for the baby shower, not price garage sale paraphernalia, nor discuss my sex life. I shouldn't be doing this. This is your moment."

Mindy settled herself comfortably in a chair and sighed happily. "I'm sure you want to have your dramatic 'Let's think about Mindy' moment, but let me tell you, I would rather find out why you disappeared last night."

Thinking about last night, Gillian frowned. "No, you wouldn't."

Mindy leaned closer with an evil grin on her face. "Trust me. I would. Was it awe-inspiring? Did the angels sing? Did the pavement melt?"

Truth, lie or hedge? "It was awful," she replied, some combination of all three.

Mindy covered her ears. "Okay. I don't want to hear this. Good gawd almighty, if a girl can't live out vicarious sexual fantasies through her bestest and most single friend, then what's the point in having high-maintenance friends?"

Determined to appear unmoved by the more painful aspects of reality, Gillian pulled out a pen and her engraved notepad and then shifted expectantly toward Mindy.

"Maybe he thinks I'm too high maintenance." Gillian considered it, wrote H.M. on the paper in neat, curlicue letters directly underneath the embossed GILLIAN H. WANAMAKER.

Mindy grabbed the pen away and scratched it out. "That's just sad. Pull your head out, silly Gilly." Then she paused, a bemused expression on her face. "You know, I have been waiting my entire life to say that, and never could. Until now."

Now properly put in her place, Gillian wrote *C-A-K-E* in bold letters on the paper. "You're exactly right. What kind of cake do you want? Red velvet, double chocolate fudge or coconut?"

"Coconut. Boiled icing."

"I told him he had to fix the rail route," Gillian explained, while writing down Mindy's preferences, not that she couldn't recite them by heart, but sometimes things needed to be put in writing.

"Maybe some fudge. No punch. I always hated punch." Mindy watched Gillian take careful notes and then glanced up. "The rail route needs fixing?"

Gillian contemplated her best "gonna pop any second now" friend and weighed the idea of unloading all of Gillian's troubles and woes on a woman who by all rights should be eating ice cream and stenciling a toy train border around a nursery ceiling. No, she would not be that heartless. "Can we talk about your baby shower for a second?"

"You're right, of course. Coconut. Fudge. No punch." Mindy paused. "Why does it need fixing?"

Realizing that her best friend was bound and determined to sidetrack the conversation, Gillian whipped out the morning edition and pointed to the minuscule newspaper article. It was a mere one column inch that might as well have said: TIN CUP'S *APOCALYPSE NOW*.

Quickly Mindy scanned the piece, then looked up and frowned. "When did this happen?"

"Yesterday."

Normally a very peaceful person, Mindy slapped a hand at the paper, a dramatic gesture most likely learned from Gillian. "Did he do this? He did this, didn't he? That tick-infested, scumball viper!"

Gillian winced. "His girlfriend did it."

Mindy tossed the paper aside. "Girlfriend? What the hell, Gillian! What the hell is wrong with you?"

It was the sort of straight-shooter thinking that was exactly what Gillian needed. Someone to make her see sense. Someone to keep her from falling into the same weak-knee trap that she laughed about in others. Not laughing to be cruel, more to feel good that she had enough self-confidence not to get that way herself. "She's not exactly his girlfriend. She's the governor's daughter. I don't think there's any deep feelings involved, more gratuitous sex," she explained, sounding exactly like everyone she'd ever laughed at. Irony was a cruel, cruel thing.

Mindy folded her arms over the bowling ball of her belly, "Oh, boo hoo, look at Mary Sue."

Gillian sniffed. "You don't have to be mean."

At that, Mindy burst out laughing and then stopped when she noticed Gillian's frankly peeved expression. "I'm sorry," she apologized, wiping the tears of laughter from her eyes. "So why aren't you charging down to the statehouse and taking care of it yourself, exactly as you've always done?"

Gillian considered the idea. "I wouldn't charge to the statehouse. This isn't baking or domestic disputes, or rounding up stray livestock. It's politics." Not that she couldn't do it if she put her mind to it, though. State politics? How hard could it be?

"Then why drag Austen into this at all?" Mindy asked, obviously believing that Gillian had some deep-seated, long-repressed lovesick motives at work.

Gillian rolled her eyes, not understanding why Mindy was overlooking the obvious. "Because it's his mess to clean up."

After Gillian stated the obvious reason, Mindy arched a brow that was soaring in its skepticism. "The real reason?"

Now that she'd been outed, Gillian stayed quiet for a minute, forming a coherent answer. "He's smarter than you think. He can do it. I'm right about this, Mindy, I know I am, and don't snicker."

Thankfully, Mindy did not snicker. "You want this for him or you? Does it tweak that legendary Gillian Wanamaker pride that you're hot for a man who most of the town considered white trash rather than some political giant with highways named after him?"

He'd never been white trash. Not to her. "You make me sound like a snob."

"No, you're a realist, and I can't figure out why you're sounding so mushy now. That is too important. What if he doesn't fix it, Gillian? What if this mess is beyond repair? Do you know what will happen then?"

Gillian tried to smile. "I'm thinking you're going to tell me."

"Damn straight. If this doesn't get set back to rights, we'll lose the station and you'll have damaged Austen's delicate psyche irrevocably—that means forever in case you're confused. Then everybody in this town will be questioning your judgment, which means you'll be back sharpening pencils at the bank while Mr. McIcky will be undressing you with his tiny rat eyes. Your mother will start baking more, then you'll eat more. You'll stop running and eventually get fat. And I, your best friend and mother of your future godchild, will have to move to Plano, where I will wither away among all the other soccer moms, blowing out my hair, taking yoga classes and drinking chardonnay. I hate chardonnay. It's like drinking ant piss."

"Why will you be in Plano?" asked Gillian, leap-frogging to the pertinent part of the conversation.

"Brad thinks the high school is going to axe some teachers. Namely him. With the baby on the way, he thought it'd be smart to move to a place with a little more job security. I had convinced him that with the rail hub and the new development plans that come along with it, we'd make it okay in Tin Cup."

Oh. "That's why you've been putting off painting the nursery?"

"The Realtor said that toy trains are a real-estate don't."

Gillian eyed her "about to pop" best friend, now realizing that life well and truly sucked for everybody in this town, and Mindy should have shared her suckiness with Gillian. "Why didn't you tell me?"

"I didn't want to say anything because I thought this was a crisis we had averted." Mindy shrugged. "Guess not."

No. It was merely a detour on the lifelong journey to Gillian getting everything that she always wanted and/ or deserved.

Her mind whirling, Gillian tapped her pen on the

paper, the light of battle in her eyes. "You and my future godchild are going nowhere. And Brad's not going
anywhere, either. I don't know how yet, but I can fix
this."

Mindy sighed with relief. "I knew you could, Gillian. I'm just not willing to leave my family's financial
well-being in the unreliable hands of Austen Hart."

Gillian, who had only last evening left her physical
well-being in the very reliable hands of Austen Hart,
wisely chose not to respond.

He would fix it. They would fix it. She would be
on him like glue until all was right, and it would be
because Gillian performed the impossible on a daily
basis. Feeling better, she shot Mindy her bestest, most
confidentest Wanamaker smile and double-checked the
list, because a woman lived and died by her ability to
throw the perfect party.

"Okay, so, we have coconut, fudge, no punch. And
how about one of those watermelon baby baskets? I can
put some lace around the edges."

"Add cherries. I used to hate cherries, but the hormones are making the taste buds wonky. Does your
momma have any fresh cherries in the kitchen? I'm
getting a little hungry." Mindy didn't wait for a response,
but instead went to forage for food, while Gillian made
goofy baby shower doodles.

It would work out. It had to.

AUSTEN TOOK THE NEWS of her accompanying him to
Austin unsurprisingly well.

"This isn't about you," she warned, seeing the leap
of anticipation in his face when she told him. And it
wasn't.

She stalked about his hotel room like a caged animal,

not that she felt the room was too small, not like she was achingly aware of the male testosterone that was flirting with her nose. "This is about Mindy's nursery and dislike of chardonnay," she continued on, valiantly ignoring it all.

"Are you going to tell me what that means?" he asked, crossing his hands behind his head, leaning back on the bed, the very picture of a man with absolutely nothing to lose. The very picture of trouble. Regretfully, she looked away.

"We need to stay focused on developing a plan, and genius takes time."

"You're too stressed. It's late. Genius doesn't appear on demand. Better to relax and let your creative juices work their magic."

"Are you propositioning me? Now?" Perhaps she was being overly sensitive, but she didn't want her magic worked. Frankly, her magic was worked enough.

"Well, I wasn't, but if you want me to, I will."

She was bone-deep tired, and Austen looked so comfortable, so easy, so tempting. Even the bed of the Spotlight Inn looked—adequate. Saliva pooled in her mouth, embarrassing her.

His eyes met hers, and Gillian felt a flash of heat, the thrill of this thing between them. Lightning.

And just as quickly, the heat in his eyes was gone. "I'm trying to be on my best behavior," he told her, his voice husky and gruff. "But this is as good as it gets. You're cruising for a fall, Gillian." And he sounded a little more than sad.

Before she did something she would regret, Gillian turned away. "We'll leave in the morning, first light."

And with that, she retreated.

THE TRIP TO Austin was four hours in the car, which meant four hours to learn more about the Secret Life and Times of Austen Hart: The Post-Tin Cup Years. Partly because she was a curious person, and more precisely because Gillian firmly believed that Austen could do this, with the proper encouragement and guidance, of course, and she didn't want to be wrong.

He had always proven her wrong, and everybody had always said she was wrong, but *wrong* wasn't a word she wanted in her vocabulary. Deep down, she wanted to think there were parts to Austen Hart that stayed hidden and locked away. Parts of him that were good and tender and caring. He'd kept those parts hidden in high school, only turning them out on special moments, but the way he'd been since he'd returned, the way he had treated her, had treated everyone, made her wonder if Austen Hart had killed those parts for good.

Maybe this was wrong.

As he drove, she watched the stillness of his hands on the wheel. Frank Hart had always had the Jim Beam jitters in his hands, that awful mad-dog twitch in his cheek, but Austen had always been still as night.

"What have you been doing since high school?"

At her question, he turned, his face hidden behind dark glasses, but the smile was all practiced charm. Another thing learned in his post-Tin Cup years. She remembered the light in his face the night he had talked about prom and the hotel. The roses, the champagne, and it dawned on her that his smile had been the same.

Feeling sad and foolish, Gillian realized that the practiced charm had been there all along.

"I've been living large."

"What happened to you?"

He turned his attention back to the road, completely

unnecessary in her opinion since they were on a desolate stretch of highway and the likelihood of impending
traffic was right up there with Gillian dying her hair
black.

"Life, darling. Life happened."

It was such a pitiful answer that Gillian blew a rasp-
berry. "Does everybody fall for that stupid line of bull?"
she asked, deciding to let him in on her disapproval of
his conduct.

Austen laughed. "It's what people expect. Meaning-
less chatter because silence is awkward, and nobody
likes the gap."

"Your social skills have improved," she noted, not
exactly a compliment.

"Don't sound so surprised."

"I'm not. I'm just not sure I like it."

"You prefer the earlier version. Awkward, cowardly,
letting the world beat him on the ass?" He laughed again,
the sound as cold as the song of a crow. She shivered and
wondered what had happened in his house growing up,
and what they had all overlooked. People had felt gener-
ally that the Harts weren't any of their business. There
was a comfort in ignorance, the idea that Gillian didn't
have to work to include father Frank in her world.

"The baby-shower planning was pretty pathetic," she
admitted, deciding it was time that she brought him into
her world, as a friend and peer, not a charity case, not
a red-hot bed partner.

A man.

She waited for him to respond, to participate, to re-
ciprocate in kind, but he merely drove on in silence.
Well, hell, so he wanted to make this inclusion thing
difficult? Gillian straightened in her seat and put on
her game face.

"Mindy said Brad wants to move to Plano," she told him, not bothering to hide the disdain in her voice.

"It's not hell," he replied, surprisingly gentle for someone who didn't give two hoots about her, her friends, or her home.

"It's close," she scoffed, folding her arms across her chest.

"Am I connected to this?"

"Of course not," she lied.

He turned, gave her that soulless look, the one that she hated. Of course, it worked. "There are jobs in Plano," she said with a sigh.

"Unlike the bustling metropolis of Tin Cup? I'm sorry, Gillian."

She heard the guilt in his voice, and it bothered her. Bad things seemed to follow Austen like a cloud. To be fair, yes, some of them he deserved, but not everything. "I could blame you for the economic woes of downtrodden little communities across this great county, but I think I'd be overstating your part in the problem. Besides, it's nothing that can't be corrected."

And just like that, just when she tried to say something nice, the chameleon was back. He flashed her a grin, the one that made women swoon. "We'll see, sugar."

"Can you not call me sugar?" she asked, trying not to sound irritated when on any other day, from any other man, she wouldn't care. But today, from him, it grated, and she knew that he knew it, and she knew that he was doing it to make her not like him, and it made her wonder why.

"I considered sugar-tits, but thought that was a little crass."

Oh, he was making this difficult. Did she care why?

She didn't need to care why. "Your daddy called me that. Once."

It was true, Frank Hart had yelled it out to her, right after she'd been elected to the sheriff's department. After his name-calling, she had made a perfect line of shotgun holes in his beloved ol' rusted Ford pick-up. Frank Hart had never called her sugar-tits again.

Austen's smile wavered. "That never came from me."

"I didn't think it did. You were too closed-mouthed to be telling tales. Besides, everybody knew how you felt about the old man."

He kept his eyes straight ahead, and his voice was flat. "Then you know why I had to leave."

"Why don't you tell me?"

He flipped on the radio station, static filling the air.

Gillian wasn't intimidated. She knew what this was about. "Is this one of those awkward silences where you're supposed to start cracking sexist blonde jokes?"

"Did you hear the one about the cheerleader—" He took a look at her face, and wisely shut up.

"Silence never bothered me," she continued, perfectly content to do whatever she needed to for however long it took. She had a captive audience for the next four hours.

Austen finally broke down and chuckled. "No, you could out-sway, out-talk anybody."

Not you, she thought. "What sort of lobbying do you do?"

"I hang out in seedy bars and pass envelopes full of cash." He didn't sound proud, didn't sound pleased, more defiant. Daring her to make a judgment.

"No hookers?" she asked, not meaning to be shallow and judgmental, not wanting to believe the worst, but this was Texas after all. Precedent was there.

"You worried that's what this will come down to? Hookers and bribes?"

"Nah." Then she frowned. "I don't want to get you in more trouble than you're already in."

He touched her hand, a small tap on the wrist, but it made her smile. "I was making a joke."

"You think we can do this?"

"Not a chance in hell."

"That's a joke, too?"

Slowly he shook his head no, the endless highway stretched out in front of them. Miles to go, and for what?

Hell.

AUSTEN BOOKED HER a room at the Driskill. Four stars and fancy roses for Gillian. It was ten years too late, but he didn't tell her that.

When they walked into the towering lobby, she oohed and aahed over the marble columns, the stained glass windows and the fashionable Victorian furnishings. Her eyes were big as stars, and he told himself he hadn't done it to impress her.

Oh, yeah, right.

The room was on the eighth floor and he lugged her bag upstairs because the bellman looked shifty and Austen knew from personal experience that Gillian was an easy mark.

While she was pondering the up-close-and-personal view of the capitol building, Jack Haywood finally deigned to return his call.

"I was wondering if you were going to thank me or throw me to the wolves."

"Aw, Jack…" Austen laughed into the phone. "The wolves would mess up that pretty face of yours, and then, well, you'd just be another sad number on the Texas unemployment line. I've got a bigger heart than that."

"No, you don't, you worthless hack. What did you want?"

Austen looked over at Gillian and gave her a "don't shoot me" wink. "I got a hot blonde who wants to see how the movers and shakers live. She wants to see the sausage factory that we call statehouse politics."

"A female, huh? Is she a professional hit lady, hired just because you're pissed? No, wait. If she's hot, I don't care."

Austen laughed his good ol' boy laugh. "I didn't think you would. We used to go to high school together, and I was giving her the business on what a lobbyist does and I might have exaggerated things a bit—"

"The size of your tool?"

"I knew you'd been looking in the men's room."

"Don't tease me, Austen. So I'm supposed to make you look good so that you can get laid?"

"Yeah, that's pretty much the story. I was greasing the skids, talking about my copious amounts of political suction, possibly mentioning that I could just snap my fingers and get anything I wanted."

"And she bought it all?"

"I'm a really good liar, Jack."

"Don't I know it, but that's not why you want to talk to me. What are you really after?"

"Railroad tracks. She loves the trains."

"Hell, Austen. Do you know how much ass-kissing I did to make Carolyn happy? And did I get laid? No. I got a freaking invite to green bean salad at the Governor's mansion. Goddamn rabbit food. So, now, you want me to go and take back all my marbles, just so you can get laid? Do I look that stupid?"

"Oh, come on, Jack."

"No. You're not getting crap from me, my friend," he said with a soft chuckle, but Austen didn't miss the hard note in his voice.

"You got some skin in this game?"

"You really want to know?"

Austen laughed. "Hell, Jack. You're the master. The man I want to emulate when I get old and flabby and wind up wearing mismatched socks."

Jack was quiet for a second and Austen wondered if he'd overplayed his hand. It was always a careful dance. A little bit of bullshit, a little bit of steel. Eventually Jack answered.

"I tell you what, and I'm only doing this because I feel sorry for you and I know women don't treat you nicely. You bring the blonde out to Bobby Trasker's barbecue tonight. I'll make you look good."

Gillian was watching him, disapproving, but still willing to wade into the mud. He only hoped it was worth it. "And the railroad?"

Jack chuckled, and Austen's heart fell at the sound, but he kept the smile on his face. "You think I can unscratch four state legislator's backs, revoke one prison contract and ungrease three new developments in environmentally sensitive areas of Houston, all in one night?"

Austen made himself chuckle. "Guess not. Guess you're just not that good. I'll have to find me another mentor to learn from."

"You are one vile S.O.B."

"Yeah. I know," Austen answered softly. Bullshit and steel. Whatever it took.

THAT AFTERNOON Austen's phone rang nonstop and Gillian found a certain morbid fascination in watching him work.

"Hey, stranger. How's it going?" he said, as he and Gillian were walking out to retrieve the car.

Gillian soon found a cute sofa and sat down in the lobby because Austen had winked at her, held up a wait-a-minute finger, and then started to chat. The man could talk. And talk. And never say anything at all. Amazing.

"How's Edie?"

Edie? Enquiring about someone's well-being? That was new. Obviously this was someone important. Restlessly she crossed one leg over the over, heel bouncing to the beat of a symphonic Beatles tune that was filtering through the lobby speakers.

"Eight hours of surgery?" he was saying, and Gillian looked over, more than a little concerned at someone being in surgery that long, but Austen was still wearing his life-is-beautiful grin.

Noticing her curious expression, he moved behind the marble column and pitched his voice lower, but Gillian was in law enforcement and believed that supersonic hearing was a job requirement. Her mother called it being nosy, but Gillian wisely dismissed that.

Idly Gillian laid her arm across the carved back of the sofa, cocking her head to one side in order to further her hearing abilities.

"I don't know when I'll be up to New York, Ty. Yeah. I signed the papers yesterday. Town was great. Same little speck on the map. I had pie at Dot's and she didn't even recognize me. Started flirting. Dude, it freaked me out."

Ty? Gillian's mind leaped to the obvious. Tyler Hart?

Deciding that polite discretion was not the be-all, end-all that her mother believed, Gillian rose and came to stand next to him so that he couldn't mistake her interest in the conversation.

"Gotta go," he said to the cell, "The ladies are calling. Hang loose, bro."

After he hung up, he blinked at her innocently, but she knew that clueless bimbo look. She had perfected the clueless bimbo look and she was no clueless bimbo, and neither was he.

"That was your brother?"

He nodded once, and some of the cluelessness fell from his eyes.

"I thought he was at Huntsville. The state Pen. The newspaper said drugs. Crystal meth. They said he had some trailer in Lockhart that exploded when he was cooking, blinding one old man in the process. An army vet."

Probably to tick her off even more, he flipped on his sunglasses. Boldly she flipped them off, tapping the overpriced pair of designer shades against her thigh.

Austen stayed silent, but his eyes were furious with her. That made two of them, because right then, she was furious with herself.

"Austen, where is your brother?" she asked, in a calm voice, a patient voice, a voice that bore no hints of impending bodily harm.

"New York."

"Is he currently a convicted felon, or has he ever

been incarcerated by the state of Texas or any other government entity?"

"No."

"Has he ever been involved in the drug trade?"

Austen smiled, hard. "Sometimes he prescribes them."

She rolled his answers over and over in her mind, and there was only one conclusion.

There are moments, humbling moments when the brain clicks to some new, revised reality where the Wizard is nothing more than a short little egomaniac, where Sweet Valley High is not a true and accurate accounting of anyone's high school years or the times in a criminal investigation where the most likely suspect is not necessarily guilty.

Her stomach pitched to a new low level. It was a reptilian feeling, like crawling, your belly scraping the ground. "Is Tyler in the medical profession? Ambulance driver? EMT?" There was a hint of desperation in her voice, a please-don't-let-me-have-screwed-up-that-badly tone. She tried to remember Tyler Hart, but she could only picture a somber face that most people said covered a criminal mind that was Godfather-like in its brilliance.

Austen laughed at her. Laughed. At. Her. "He's a cardiothoracic surgeon, living in Manhattan, and he's got four surgical procedures named after him. They're working on an off-line heart pump for transplants, plan to patent it next year, but I'm not supposed to know about that, so you can't tell."

Gillian stared, open-mouthed, and more than a little upset that he hadn't bothered to educate her on the actual truth of this matter.

His finger lifted her chin, closing her jaw, and then he plucked his sunglasses from her lifeless hand.

"Ready to go, sugar?"

Oh, hell, no. She was not going anywhere. Not yet.

Heels clicking on marble, she ran after him and grabbed the back of his suit jacket, stopping him in his tracks.

"Why didn't you say anything?"

Austen stared, stonewall calm, and she could feel the accusations shooting from every pore of his taut body. Often being on the judgy end of the interrogation process herself, Gillian immediately recognized the look. It wasn't fun.

"Did you care, Gillian? You don't even remember my brother."

"Vaguely," she replied, not bothering to defend herself, not really deserving to, but he should have told her. "You should have told me. You could have told me."

"The other night I saw you for the first time in ten years. We didn't have a lot of time for words." It was a crude insult. And it hurt.

Gillian stomped on his foot. Hard. And was somewhat pleased with his quiet *oof* of pain. "You will not be a jackass. Not now. Did you think I wouldn't have believed you?"

"Would you, Gillian? Would you really?" He didn't bother to answer his own question, but walked briskly to the valet, as if he couldn't bear her company.

While the nice young valet tucked her into her seat, Gillian quietly seethed, steeped in guilt and frustration and the heavy knowledge that she had made a serious mistake, and she had hurt him in the process.

The quiet engine rumbled to life, and they pulled out onto the avenue, a glorious summer day, but she didn't have the heart to appreciate it. "I think I would have believed you," she said quietly. "Now, granted, a career choice that was a bit more modest might have been easier…."

"I could tell you he's in retail. Is that easier?"

Oh, he was mad, she could see it steaming off him, his jaw tight, his face flushed, but fury was so much easier for her to handle than pain. Especially pain that she had caused. "Is he in retail?"

He slapped a hand on the wheel. Real anger. Honest anger. Tyler was a sore spot. Oh, sure, people could think Austen was the son of Satan himself. Why, he'd pull out his pitchfork and his oh-sugar wink to prove it, but his brother? His brother walked on cardiothoracic water.

Gillian tucked away that knowledge.

"I would have believed you," Gillian said, her voice low.

Austen glanced over, his sunglasses firmly in place. "Why should you?" Then he shook his head. "Why does it matter?"

"It matters to me. It obviously matters to you, so let's not lie about that. Why didn't you tell me about him? What did he do after he left town?"

It took another three minutes before she finally convinced him to trust her. As they drove along the highway, she listened to him talk about his brother, about how Tyler had been the smart one to think ahead, to plan to get out right from the start. Leaving Austen alone. He left out that part, glossed over it with jokes and spin. But Gillian knew better. Then he talked about Tyler going to med school, Tyler growing into a world-class surgeon. She heard the pride in Austen's voice. Pride for Tyler, but never himself. She tucked that little bit of info away, too. The Saturday traffic was heavy due to road construction, but she didn't mind the delay. It was a chance for her to learn.

Once off the freeway, the houses changed from modest brick to palatial Texas palaces, hidden behind automatic gates, and emerald green lawns. Austen pulled into a long driveway where efficient young boys in tuxedos collected keys and directed traffic. Gillian noted the white stone mansion with its formal white columns, its wraparound porch and the state flag flying high and proud from the flagpole in the yard.

When she was in high school, she would have given her eyeteeth to live in such a house, but not now. She studied Austen as he emerged from the car, but he wasn't showing anything at all. She took his arm, noted the tense muscles underneath the elegant suit. "I'm sorry. I leap to assumptions faster than most superheroes can fly. Sometimes those assumptions are wrong."

He nodded once. "Maybe I should have said something, but I didn't want to know."

She stopped, let a well-dressed couple pass by them, and then tugged at his arm. "Know what?"

He hesitated. "If you would believe me. I didn't want to know."

Touched by the admission, Gillian reached out and took his hand. He let her, and for a minute they stood in the middle of the sidewalk, amidst the fragile blooms of heirloom roses, and Gillian realized he'd let her see. Only a flash, only a hint, but he'd trusted her.

Grateful for that, she gave him her best smile. It wasn't the "aren't you special" smile, not the "let's all remain calm" smile, but a real and true smile that few ever saw. A wavering smile full of all the uncertainty that she never showed.

"You ready for this?" he asked, nodding toward the heavy oak door with its lion head knocker. A lion's head? Pretentious much?

He slid his sunglasses in his pocket, then straightened his tie, and she shooed his hands away, showing him how sartorial perfection was done. "You look great," she told him, daring to press a kiss to his cheek.

"You can't act too smart," he warned, as if she was a moron.

She fluttered her lashes shamelessly. "Now, honey. Don't act like I haven't lived in this state my entire life. A little leg, a wide-eyed smile, witty repartee, but never enough brain to wither a manhood. They are so fragile, you know."

His mouth curved and he kissed her once, full of awe and all the respect she deserved, and she felt the prickles run through her, all the way down to her toes. It wasn't fair that Austen Hart was the one man that could do this to her. Not fair at all.

THE SWEEPING expanse of backyard was filled with Texas politicians. Austen scanned the layout, noticing who was talking to whom, taking a hard look at who seemed worried, who seemed happy, and the most vulnerable of all: those who seemed a little too happy.

Budget season was never pretty, and this year had been especially contentious. Two weeks ago, the governor had called the legislators back, and now Austin was swarming with sweaty statesmen and women who really wanted to be at home campaigning for the fall elections.

"Is that the governor?" Gillian whispered, nodding toward Miles Carver, who seemed remarkably cool for a man in a suit and tie.

"That's him. Want to meet him?"

She thought for a moment, and then shook her head. "Not yet. Can't be needy or pushy."

Austen smothered his laugh, and she shot him a sideways look, masked with a sweet smile. "Why is that funny?"

"You can be pushy sometimes."

"Pushy females are tacky. I'm not tacky."

"Threatening to shoot a tire is pushy."

She drew herself up to her full height, which almost reached his shoulder. Almost. "I considered that a justified use of force. It worked."

Right then, out of the corner of his eye, Austen noticed Jack Haywood in deep, no doubt diabolical discussions on the far patio. There were four state reps surrounding him, two looking happy, and two looking miffed. Austen noted the two miffed ones. Fred Templeton from Fort Worth, and Sherry Hunter from El Paso. In state dealings, El Paso was never happy, sort of the bastard child in the money chain, but Austen knew Rep. Hunter was new to the capital and still believed in the concept of honest government. She would be perfect.

Fred was a harder sell, but he and the governor never saw eye to eye. He could be turned. "We start by throwing a little monkey wrench in the budget vote. It's the governor's first priority, and he'll do a lot to get it passed. We take away two votes, come to the governor and tell him that we can get two back. It's the leverage we need to reopen the negotiations on the rail route."

Gillian noticed where he was looking. "Those two? I love her dress. I think it's Chanel. Two years ago, the spring line."

She saw his surprised expression and shrugged. "I

always talk fashion when my nerves get jittery. It's sort of a default reflex."

It was nice to see Gillian nervous. It made her seem more real, more human…*more possible*.

No.

After clearing his brain of such possibilities, Austen rolled his eyes in mock exasperation. "As long as it's not hair."

She stroked his arm in mock seduction. "You don't mind taking me to Armands to get my highlights done, do you, you big ol' studmuffin?"

Not waiting for his answer, she headed for the first two targets. In two minutes flat, Gillian had made plans for a shopping trip with Rep. Hunter and emailed a copy of her secret rib recipe to Rep. Templeton.

Why was he even surprised?

Austen sidled up to Fred. "Hey, Fred? Can I talk to you for a minute?" he asked, pulling the man aside. Next, Austen plucked a glass of whiskey from a passing waiter and then swirled the ice, pretending to be deep in thought.

Templeton was a more seasoned politician, but even so, his long, thin face grew worried. "Something wrong?"

Austen stared up at the sky, pursed his lips and sighed. "No, Fred, actually it's something that I think you're gonna like." He looked back at the man, weighing his trustworthiness. "You can't tell anybody, at least not yet, but I knew you were sweating the vote on the new defense contract in your district—"

"You know something?" asked Fred eagerly.

Austen laughed, but in a nice way. "Not about that, no, but I know you didn't want to go against the governor on the budget, but you felt, in your heart, it was the right thing to do..." Austen swore under his breath. "I can't believe they wanted to cut school funding. In this day and age?" Sorrowfully he shook his head. "Sorry, gets me all fired up just thinking about it."

Fred's earnest blue eyes narrowed. "I didn't know you cared."

Austen put his free hand to his heart. "We can't ignore the children."

After that frankly showy gesture, Fred got straight to the point. "What does this have to do with me?"

Austen worried; here he was considering the political consequences of doing the right thing for the first time in his career. Of course, he still wasn't doing the right thing. His eyes met Gillian's. But at least he was doing it for the right reasons.

"It's okay," Fred reassured him, because he was that sort of man. "You can trust me."

Austen met Fred's earnest gaze and nodded solemnly. "Miles is talking to Washington. He's thinking of taking the federal dollars. Now, you can see why he doesn't want that to get out before the election."

Fred nodded. "Political suicide."

Austen took a deep swig of whiskey, as if driven to drink by the very thought of such a kamikaze move. "Exactly, but come December, two weeks *after* the election, the jobs numbers are going to have to be—" Austen held up quote fingers "—'readjusted,' because there might have been some statistical errors in the calculations. The governor knows it, and the president, well, he's going to be his knight in shining federally mandated armor."

Fred frowned. "But what does that have to do with me?"

Austen hid his frustration. He was used to dealing

with people who knew enough to analyze every fact from their own self-interest first, before actually listening.

"The budget is moot. Shoot it down. Keep your conscience clear and your voting record clean. They like that in Fort Worth. A man with principles."

Fred considered that, and his narrow face glowed with the idea of it. The man would sleep easier tonight, and it was all because of Austen.

Austen winked at Gillian, a silent "one down" and made his way to Rep. Hunter, dumping the whiskey in a planter.

One to go.

"You're nervous."

Never liking to appear anything less than perfect, Gillian tamped down the urge to smooth her hair. "No, I'm not. I'm never nervous." In the end, she settled for the slight fluff of her ends. Because of the heat, of course. "Is it always this easy?"

He shot her a flat look. "It's never this easy. But right now it's budget season and the economy's in the toilet, and the oil industry is torn between being scared of alternative energy sources and not wanting to look too arrogant. If it wasn't this easy then I would have driven four hundred miles back here without a second thought, and you would still be in Tin Cup, arresting shoplifters and herding livestock off the highway. And in general, everybody would get screwed. Although, if you didn't have me to help, you'd still be screwed. The budget's the key to the kingdom. Once the governor thinks it's toast, he'll be ready to deal. I might not be able to make the high-dollar promises that Haywood did, but I know what the little guys want. Nobody else pays attention, but you never know when you need the little guys on your side."

Austen seemed almost proud. "You turn one state legislator, and now you're getting cocky?" she teased.

This time, yes, he was definitely proud. "It's the way you're undressing me with your eyes," he teased in return.

"Don't think I can't tell what you're thinking. I told you I wasn't here for the sex."

This time, she did smooth her hair.

They were on dangerous ground here, acting like lovers, acting like friends. It didn't feel like an act, and Gillian knew that at least on her part it wasn't an act.

Languidly, Austen looked her over, dark eyes lingering, and she could feel the tightness in her stomach, the heat between her thighs. "Your mouth says no, but I wonder what parts are currently saying yes?"

She managed a sophisticated tinkle of laughter. "Is this what power does to a man? Make him stupid and horny?"

"The two words are redundant." He pushed back the hair from her face, an odd, gentle gesture for a womanizing lady-killer. "Are you having a good time?"

Gillian cleared her throat, pretending she wasn't affected. "It's a nice party. The canapés are to die for. I got the recipe from the chef. I'm thinking I'll surprise Mindy with them at the shower."

From across the lawn, she could see the elegant brunette with mile-high legs that she probably spread like...

No, no, no.

"She keeps staring at you," Gillian muttered, not wanting to sound jealous, but still sounding jealous. Not that she wanted to be jealous of a...

No, no, no.

"Ignore her," Austen instructed, sipping at his beer, yet studiously, suspiciously avoiding the other woman's attention.

"I want to ignore her, but eventually you will have to converse and likely she doesn't handle awkward social situations with any sort of grace and polish, and I—"

Austen lifted her hand, turned her palm out, and kissed her wrist. It was elaborate, showy, possessive and more than a bit sexy. Gillian felt the blush in every inch of her body. "That was not necessary."

He looked smug and manly. "I know."

On the other side of the lawn, Carolyn Carver was still watching them, all pouty smiles and bedroom eyes that most men seemed to go for. Gillian pushed her hair back, and smiled politely in return.

This was the way women fought in this state: lipstick, compliments and a dash of hemlock splashed in sweet tea.

"I want to meet her," Gillian whispered in his ear, accidentally brushing her lips over the warmth of his skin. He shivered. She noticed. So did Carolyn Carver, and Gillian knew she was in for trouble because the woman's dress was couture, and that wasn't cubic zirconia that dangled from her ears.

Austen, not sensing the territorial undercurrents, pulled her behind the roses. "Don't waste your time on something that doesn't matter."

He seemed unmoved, but that was the problem. "Doesn't anything matter to you anymore? You used to care, you used to feel."

He smiled at her, careless and cool. "Not me. Not ever."

"They why are we here?"

"Can't figure that one out, can you?" His hand slid over her bare arm, and suddenly she wasn't sure what was pretend and what was real. Conscious of a thousand prying eyes, Gillian pulled him beyond the high row of roses.

She searched his face, looking for some sign of caring. "It's the right thing to do. It's a good thing, and an honorable thing, and you don't have to lie and pretend that it's only lust that is driving you."

His eyes flickered, there was a softening in his mouth, but then from a thousand miles away someone laughed, loud and rough, and Austen held her against him.

His mouth covered hers like a man without a country, his tongue sliding boldly between her lips. His hands slipped beneath her dress, pulling her tight to his body, letting her feel the thick length of his erection, fitting himself snugly between her thighs as if she was nothing more than a thing.

His kiss was crude, pillaging and raiding like a destroyer intent on burning the land. Stupid with fury, her hand raised, ready to slap, ready to hurt.

But something stopped her just in time. Beneath her thin dress, beneath the veneer of his suit, she could feel the beat of his heart—rabbit scared.

Her fingers rose, not so angry. She cupped the rigid planes of his cheeks, tender and warm, feeling his mouth gentle on hers.

At the unexpected turn, her own pulse quickened, the late-afternoon sun beating down, the fine rose scent heavy in the air. She could taste the burn of whiskey on him, the dark fire of a man who was determined to stay in hell.

Her fingers tangled in his hair, and her hips arched

against him because she wanted to feel him, and she needed to see what he would do.

Austen drew back a mere inch, his eyes heavy and black with desire. The sound of his breathing was staggered and angry, but he stayed frozen, controlled. Gently, oh-so carefully, she smiled.

Instantly his breathing calmed, and the forgotten finger slipped beneath her panties, slipping inside her. All the while he was watching her, waiting for her to fight or pull away, but she would not. Frozen and controlled she stood, her muscles clenched and tight. It was anger that was driving her, anger and lust.

While his treacherous hand played her, Gillian didn't flinch, she didn't blink, she locked her eyes with his. Back and forth he stroked, and she could feel the swelling of her flesh, the all too human moisture giving proof to his particular brand of the truth. He wanted to believe it was lust, because he was too stubborn to believe anything else.

His face was carefully still, waiting for her to break, waiting for her to come. Her muscles began to contract, and if she were a little stronger, she would have pulled away, but he expected that from her, thinking she was stronger than she really was.

With each touch of his hand, her blood throbbed, the warm sun heating her skin, and inside her, everything wanted to drift and let go. Still he watched her face, his fingers thrusting deep, his movements faster, and Gillian could feel the pressure building between her thighs.

Not willing to let him win, she locked her knees, focusing on staying upright, focusing on the single drop of sweat on his brow.

A tiny pulse in his cheek gave him away. Her muscles began to spasm and she knew he could feel the release in her, but she didn't gasp, she didn't close her eyes, and as the orgasm took over, she withstood the pressure, showing him exactly how calm and controlled were done.

Long seconds later, he withdrew from her, took a slow step back, but this time there was no patronizing wink or soulless smile. He was absolutely still, waiting for her to explode.

Efficiently she smoothed her skirt, her hands steady. When she thought her appearance was suitably restored, Gillian raised a brow. She wanted to yell at him, but she kept her voice carefully in check. "I will not let you spit on this. I will not let you spit on me, and I will not let you spit on the remaining pieces of your heart—small and pitiful as they might be. There is a state representative who is waiting to be charmed by the potency of your smile. There is a young lady, and I use that term only in the loosest sense of the word, who is waiting to see if my lipstick is smudged, or whether my dress looks especially mussed. I will not give her that satisfaction. Do I make myself clear?"

It was a rhetorical question. She didn't wait for a response because she was about to collapse. A stiff shot of whiskey was what she needed. Most of all, she was terrified that he would walk away.

So she marched off to the bar and sweet-talked the bartender out of a quick shot of whiskey. Courage now duly fortified, Gillian strolled past Carolyn Carver with her head held high. There were some women who would run away from a fight, but not Gillian. Not a fight with Austen, and not a fight with the governor's daughter, either. Carolyn might not know they were at war, but they were….

Just as she was within spitting distance, Carolyn smiled, warm and full of charity, as only Texas women can do. "Hey, sugar. Love the dress. It does great things for that sleek figure of yours, but I think the back is hanging a little off." She pitched her voice low. "You should find a mirror."

Then Gillian patted her arm just so, and headed for the ladies' room, a hidden tree, a linen closet, or pretty much anywhere else she could go and fall apart in peace.

THERE WERE FEW TIMES in his life when Austen felt shame. He spent most of his childhood pretending shame didn't exist, but once he'd finally pried himself out from under the thumb of Frank Hart, he found that life was a bottle of tequila, meant to be chugged and then tossed. The downside to tequila chugging was that each morning you woke up with a worm in your mouth.

In short, the Three Horsemen of the Apocalypse— shame, guilt and regret—were a big waste of time. Still, as he watched Gillian walk toward the house, as he watched that stiff-legged pride, he couldn't help but feel...well, *uncomfortable* seemed the word that he found most acceptable.

Most of him could not comprehend why she bothered with a professional liar who had a foul-mouthed drunk for a father, and a brother who apparently cooked up crystal meth when he wasn't in the operating room.

It was a good thing he'd never told her about his sister, Brooke.

Slowly he scratched his chest, his nose enamored by the lingering whiff of her wildflower perfume. His cock stiffened at the dark smell of her sex. And from his heart, from the small and pitiful pieces of his heart? He felt a distant thumping, and he told himself that he was still woozy from lust.

A few minutes later he returned to the party, potent smile back in place. There were a few judges that he slapped on the back, a few faceless wives whom he flirted with shamelessly. All while he waited breathlessly for her return.

When Gillian did emerge from the house, she stood poised in the doorway, the sun's glow glinting off her in a way he knew she had planned. Feeling the draw of his gaze, she shot him a smile that was full of triumph and innocence, of sins not forgiven and tears that would never be shed.

From deep within his chest, the small and pitiful pieces of his heart coughed and sputtered, angry at being disturbed from their rest.

There was nothing that would ever come of this, since he could never be the man she hoped he was, but Austen Hart was damn good at playing the game, and for a few days—a few glorious days—he would.

8

GILLIAN LAUGHED AND told stories, and listened with awestruck eyes to every elected official she met. There was one state senator, a very soft-spoken young man, who explained in great length about the tragic plight of the brown-backed scorpions who were being chased farther from their native habitat by the callous developers who thought nothing of squishing them like bugs.

As he talked on, she noticed the abundance of limestone on the garden wall. She squinted carefully because if perchance she ever did see a scorpion, that bugger was toast.

Austen, perhaps noticing the unattractive pallor of her skin or the glazed look in her eyes that seemed at odds with her mission, gallantly appeared to rescue her.

"I need to introduce you to Jack," he told her as they strolled across the lawn. "I put it off as long as I could, but he thinks he's the reason we're here, and I don't want him to think otherwise and start asking questions. Are you okay with that?"

It was an odd question from a man who had made it his life's mission to disrespect her daily. His tone was gentlemanly and appropriate.

Progress had been made on the political battlefield. They now had four state legislators ready to raise up against the governor—definite progress—and there had been progress on the personal battlefield, as well.

Gillian, who had managed more victories than Alexander the Great, knew how to accept the triumph with good manners, and he was damned lucky that she noticed and had graciously chosen not to rub his nose in it.

"So Jack's the turncoat who diverted the rail route, the one who opted to destroy my town without an ounce of compassion for the people whose very existence will now be squashed like a bug?"

"Franklin was talking to you about the brown-backed scorpion?" he asked, in a completely unsurprised voice.

"At great and wearying length."

"I trust you won't feel the need to lecture Jack on his lack of compassion, nor shoot him between the eyes?"

She sighed. "You sure do know how to ruin a girl's fun."

At her purposefully provocative words, she waited for the lewd wisecrack or the wolfish leer in his eyes, but Austen Hart only said, "Buzzkill, that's me."

They laughed and mingled and oh-so casually made their way over to Jack.

Jack Haywood looked to be in his fifties, steely gray hair, icy blue eyes and a simpering young thing who thought that a white linen dress was best worn without a bra.

"You must be Jack," Gillian said, holding out her hand, somewhat surprised that his grip wasn't clammy.

"Jack, meet Gillian, an old friend of mine from high school."

Gillian, knowing her part, acted appropriately impressed.

Jack, knowing his part, acted appropriately pleased. "I wish I'd been at your high school, Austen. Maybe my grades would have been better." He shrugged beefy shoulders. "Maybe not. How long will you be staying in town?"

Gillian turned to Austen and laughed. "Oh, who knows? I'm not big on rigid schedules and structure. You know, life is too important to put it on a timer."

Jack chuckled, then squeezed the young thing that was hanging on his arm. "That's exactly what I tell my doctor every time he wants me to give up my evening scotch. Austen says that you're fascinated with the government process and came here to check out the behind-the-scenes wheeling and dealing."

"I had a couple of civics courses in college, but it's a lot more interesting to see the way it actually plays out."

Jack looked at her oddly, and she realized a woman going to college confused him.

"I failed the classes, of course," she added with a wistful tone in her voice, and Jack and his friend laughed once again.

Austen, she noted, did not laugh, only coughed to the side.

"I saw him taking you around," Jack said, "making the introductions. I hope your time here is productive."

Productive? That was a weird, and possibly cover-blowing choice of words. Not ready to believe the worst, Gillian chuckled, shaking her hair back and forth in a carefree manner. Two seconds of silence passed before Gillian figured out that the man had expected an answer. The icy blue eyes were studying her much like developers studied the pesky brown-backed scorpion. Gillian knew that Jack Haywood was not nearly as clueless as he pretended to be, possibly because he was aware that Gillian was not nearly as clueless as she pretended to be. Although frankly, if she'd been smarter, she probably would not have rushed to judgment so fast.

Now appropriately respectful, she met his eyes. "Today wasn't nearly productive as I had hoped it would be," she told him, sounding tired and frustrated because she was.

Something passed over the man's face, something that made her skin crawl. It was then that Austen stepped in between them. "Gillian's an idealist, Jack. Don't burst her bubble too soon." He placed a protective, possessive arm around her shoulders. A very nice touch.

That was the sort of cro-magnon tactic that Jack Haywood seemed to understand best. "You should introduce her to J.C.," the man said, sensing the pesky bug had been crushed and the crisis had passed.

"Who's J.C.?" asked Gillian, in her happiest, peskiest voice.

"J. C. Travis. The railroad commissioner of this fine state. She's third in line to the governorship. I bet you two would get along fine." Then Jack turned to Austen. "J.C. will listen and smile, cluck her tongue in sympathy, and tell you how mad she is about the changed route. In the end, there's not a thing she can do about it, but you should try. I'm assuming that J.C. is next on your list?"

At the question, Gillian kept her face carefully blank. Austen's smile turned cold, much colder than she'd ever seen. There was no pretense here. That was all mean. "That's good advice," he said, the cold smile staying put. "I knew you were my mentor for a reason."

She survived a few more minutes of strained conversation before Austen decided that they'd stayed long enough.

The fierce eyes of Jack Haywood were watching her take her leave, but Gillian still managed to smile graciously, her hand clutching Austen's arm more firmly than she intended, but he didn't seem to mind. "Good to meet you, Jack," she said, because certainly, the man had taken the gloves off, but there was no reason to forget good breeding.

He nodded. "Always a pleasure when a beautiful woman graces us with her company. Austen's sticking his neck out awfully far for you, Miss Wanamaker. I hope tonight you'll be appropriately grateful."

Underneath her hand, she felt Austen's muscle tense, but he was foolish if he thought a few adolescent remarks were going to move her to violence. There were so many more options.

She laughed then, because when in over your head, confident superiority worked best. "Mr. Haywood, I'm not exactly sure what your idea of gratitude entails, and I'm not sure my feeble brain can comprehend all these subtle nuances. Regrettably, I think you're saying that appropriate gratitude involves sucking a man's balls until his head explodes, and let me clarify, I'm referring to the little head rather than the big head, in case you were confused by the subtle nuances between those two. I'm surprised you don't know that there are people who indulge in sexual congress because they like each other, are attracted to each other, and possibly respect each other, too. Let me tell you something, there are women who actually bed a man because they want to, rather than because they *owe* him."

Jack's eyes narrowed to mere slits, and he started to

speak, but she held up a finger and turned to his companion. "I don't know what you *owe* him, but take it from me, even the promise of world peace isn't enough." Unable to help herself, she nodded at the woman's chest. "And buy a bra. That's just tacky."

With those parting words, she and Austen walked off.

"*Tell me* I didn't ruin it. We only have three days to change their minds before the governor's press conference. And I think I ruined it." Gillian was currently sitting on her hotel bed, her head in her hands, nursing the mother of all morning-after regrets.

Austen tried to comfort her, albeit pointlessly, and they both knew it.

"You didn't ruin it." He sounded so earnest, so sincere, she had to look up and see who was actually speaking.

Noting the hard truth on his face, she swore. "You're such a liar."

"Hey, it's not a huge surprise that Jack would figure out that if we can't get the route changed through the front door, then we'll try to change it through the back."

"Which we're going to change," she corrected.

"Which we're trying to change," he corrected, and she let it slide only because there were bigger things to worry about. Namely, her mouth. "But if he's right about J.C., we were screwed before we started."

"Are we going to meet her?"

"Yeah. I called her last night. I can't go to my boss for help with this one, but I can go to her. If we jam up the budget vote, I'll need to dole out some favors, and J.C. likes to play Santa Claus."

"And Jack can stop all this?"

Austen shrugged. "I don't know."

She buried her head in her hands. "I should have kept my mouth shut."

"Don't worry about it." The words rolled off his tongue because no, he had never shot off his mouth and ruined things. "So what if Jack found out that I wanted to torpedo the budget process. Who cares? Yes, it was earlier than might be strategically advantageous, but when life hands you shit…" He stopped, frowned.

"What?" she asked, curious.

"Nothing."

"No, finish it. When life hands you shit, you what? Fertilize the roses, turn it into organic fuel?"

"No. You open a new bottle and get yourself good and drunk."

She pushed herself up from the bed, wondering if everyone was right about Austen. Maybe it was pointless. A fool's errand, but dammit, Gillian wasn't wrong. She couldn't be. Why couldn't he see what she saw in him? Right now, he was her only hope, and to be perfectly honest, she wished he would put more effort into the process. "That's your idea of positive platitudes?"

"It's better than what Frank always said."

Hearing that, Gillian glanced over, surprised at Austen's words, but it was safer to stay casual, make a joke, as if discussing Frank Hart was everyday conversation. Like the weather.

"What did Frank—" she started, her voice light, and then held up a hand. "No, I don't want to know."

He hadn't noticed, his face distracted. There was a tension in his shoulders, his jaw tight, and as she paced around the room, his eyes followed her, filled with something primal. Something predatory. Something that made her body yearn. After a few moments, he stood. "Let's go eat."

Food? The man wanted food? Now? When she had other...more stimulating ideas? "How can you be hungry? I'm too wound up to eat. That smarmy bastard, Haywood. God, it's like he oozes instead of walks. I don't know how you can do this all the time without needing some antivenom vaccine."

"I take a lot of showers," Austen answered, sounding as if he were serious.

She looked wistfully in the direction of the bathroom. "I think a shower is a top-shelf idea."

At her suggestion, his skin turned pinkish pale, and Austen Heartless Womanizing Whore-Dog Hart studiously inspected the color of his sapphire blue tie.

Gillian was intrigued. So the idea of a shower was making him nervous? Fascinated by the contradiction, Gillian smiled to herself. "We'll do dinner, and figure out the best way to play it with J.C., but let me get cleaned up first. You don't mind, do you?"

He looked as if he'd rather be scraping up roadkill, but he nodded like a trooper. Gillian opened the closet and pulled out a dress. The perfect black chiffon with the swirling skirt and the classically low halter neckline. Elegant, sophisticated, it screamed "I want to have sex." Discreetly, of course.

Holding it up in front of her, she moved to the mirror. For a second she met his dark eyes, and felt the temperature shoot up a hundred degrees. In the end, it was her gaze that slid away although her heart seemed a little fascinated by the game.

Avoiding the danger in his direction, she grabbed fresh underthings and escaped to the bathroom because she had trusted Austen Hart more times than she could count, and she wasn't quite ready to trust him again. No matter how much she wanted to.

SEX WAS NOT SOMETHING that Austen usually struggled with. He believed in it, knew the medical benefits of it, really enjoyed it, and although perhaps he couldn't satisfy a woman emotionally, for a good hour, sometimes four, he could make sure that woman had a heullva good time. He'd never done that with Gillian, not once.

From the bathroom, he could hear the sounds of Gillian getting naked, Gillian soaping some sort of bubbly gel stuff over that soul-stealing body. He could hear her fingers skimming over her soft skin, the wet slide of her body against the tiles. Most devastatingly of all, he could hear the quiet moans as she made herself come.

No, Gillian Wanamaker would not pleasure herself in a shower. Most likely—because he had given the matter some amount of thought—she would have a vibrator that she kept tucked away in her closet behind her Lionette cheerleader uniform. When the house was quiet and the town at rest, she would lay herself down on the bed, spread her legs only just enough, and then after all the lights were off, she would turn on the radio. George Strait's smooth voice would fill the air. Then, with no one to see, she would touch herself gently, a small smile on her lips.

Her hands would trail over her breasts, light as a feather, amused by the idea of a good girl gone bad. Then, because Gillian Wanamaker did nothing half measure, she would move on to serious fondling of the pair of rosy-tipped nipples. The night air would dampen her skin, making her body shimmer like gold. Her laughter would be smothered and soft. She would draw a quick breath, those perfect breasts rising, her fingers skimming down to the neatly trimmed curls of gold that ruled from the top of her thighs.

In the back of his mind, Austen vividly recalled Gillian Wanamaker in all her flagrant, naked glory, and *that* Gillian Wanamaker had a wax job that was as stripped as his soul. But the image of shimmering curls of gold did not go away.

With a developing problem in his pants, Austen moved to the window, farther away from the nonexistent sounds in the bathroom, but the images in his brain played on, the sounds continued to mock his ears.

Austen had always floated fluidly between reality and fantasy. Sometimes there was no reason. Sometimes it kept him sane, but he always knew that the fantasy did not exist, and to actually begin to trust in fantasy now was a stunningly bad idea.

Gillian was a fantasy.

He repeated the words aloud in case his mind wasn't paying attention.

"Were you talking to me?"

Fantasy, shithead.

"Were you talking to me?"

His fantasy repeated the words, and Austen turned because it was the only way to get it through his brickwall of a brain that…

Shit.

She was wrapped in a hotel towel, standing in front of the bathroom door, her hair wet and tangled, and everything about her was wrong.

Her eyes looked soft and tender and she was sucking nervously on her bottom lip—not that it wasn't an awesome lip—but the visual was off.

The visual was waiting, expecting him to speak in an intelligent manner.

"What?"

"Were you talking to me?" the visual stated.

"No." Austen jammed his hands in his pockets because he wanted to touch her, he wanted to taste her, he wanted to plunge his cock inside the luminous image in front of him, and he knew that was wrong. Every time he touched her, he destroyed her. Ergo, no touching, which was easy because she didn't exist. She was a fantasy.

"Who were you talking to?" she asked, moving closer to him, and now, not only were his eyes and ears acting up, but he could smell her. Shampoo. Clean, fresh. Pure.

Austen took careful steps back to the window. For one panic-stricken moment he considered how much force it would take to dive through it, but Austen Hart had never been that brave.

Not once.

She tilted her head, and he could see the drops of water that she had missed, drops that were clinging desperately to the soft gold of her skin. He knew that feeling, the idea of clinging desperately to her, and he wanted to lick the beads of water off with his tongue.

No touching, no licking. Licking was bad.

"I was talking to myself," he replied in a completely competent voice, talking to a woman who did not exist.

"I thought I heard my name."

The towel slipped a half inch lower, now dwelling somewhere close to the Valley of Death.

The only thing he had to fear was the evil in himself.

Never in his life had he wanted anything more. His brain was screaming at him, yelling at him to jump, to pounce, to use, to toss, and it was the first time in a long, long time that he told his brain no.

She moved closer.

Austen racked his brain. All he needed were the words to make his brain shut up.

"Gillian," he said, talking to the illusion in front of him. "I'm going to ask you something and I don't mean to be rude or crude, but it's a good idea for you to tell me, because I swear that I could hear… And I knew you weren't…and it was sort of freaky and…"

"What did you hear?" the woman asked, as if he seemed perfectly sane.

"Did you touch yourself…privately, in the shower. I could hear…sounds."

She stared up at him with her brilliant blue eyes, dazzling him, hypnotizing him. "No," the visual answered, and it was the answer he needed to hear.

Fantasy. Definitely.

Austen began to breathe again.

The woman, the one who did not exist, smiled at him. "Did you want me to?"

"No," he said, his voice unnaturally loud.

The woman looked at him in amused disbelief.

That was that look in her eyes, the one that said "liar" that made all the pieces click into place.

Gillian Wanamaker was standing before him with only a towel separating her from ten years' worth of explicit dreams—none of them good.

Obviously not knowing the vile thoughts in his head, Gillian Wanamaker dropped the towel.

Shit. Shit. Shit.

Gillian Wanamaker—the naked, real Gillian Wanamaker—reached out with her very real fingers and took his face in her hands.

This was not the game. This was disaster.

"Austen," she said, speaking slowly, at last comprehending his lack of quality brain function. "Touch me."

The fantasy was back, but Austen was prepared for that trick.

"No."

She stepped closer, until their bodies were pressed together. She seemed so small, so slight, so breakable, with those delicate breasts burning into his chest like a brand. Austen closed his eyes, willing this to disappear, but when he opened them again, there she was, torturing him, seducing him, and he could feel his control slipping away. Her fingers trailed over his brows, traced the furrow in his forehead, her touch as light as a feather. It was like nothing he'd ever known.

The clear blue of her eyes shone with absolute trust, the same way she'd looked at him so long ago. "Do you want to touch me?"

His hands remained in his pockets, but Austen did nod his head yes. Just like in one of his dreams, her right hand took his left hand and joined them together. His hands were smoother now, his fingers were obsessively clean, but it still felt wrong.

She took his hand and raised it to her face. Slowly, he stroked the smooth shape of her cheek. As she guided his hand, he traced the fragile curves of her ear. Still believing in him, she moved his hand to her mouth.

While he touched her, her eyes watched him, trusting, not testing. Cautiously he followed the plump shape of her mouth, feeling the hills and the dips.

Foolishly trusting him on his own, her hand fell to her side.

The princess-blue eyes were waiting, expecting him to know what to do.

Commanding him to touch, but not like before....

Clumsy fingers slid over damp strands of her hair, through the silk and the tangles, exploring the way it brushed on her shoulder.

The shoulder seemed a deceptively safe place to be, but there were no safe havens on the body of Gillian Wanamaker. Every inch was a minefield, primed to blow up in his face. He could feel his heart hammering in his chest, primed to blow up, as well. That and his cock, but Austen continued on, too stupid to stop. As he touched her, her eyes stayed locked with his. He could still see the trust there in the endless depths, but there was doubt there, as well. Memories of all the things that he'd done to her, all the ways that he'd hurt her.

Rationally, his mind lectured him on the difference between what he could see, and what actually was. There was the pain that he believed could actually be forgotten, and the pain that never would. Realizing that the pain that he had caused her would never be forgotten, it became easier to touch her, because they were still playing the game. That was all he needed to remember. Play the game.

His hands were masterfully gentle as he learned the slender muscles of her arm, toned and strong. Like a lover, his fingertips followed the fine ridge of her spine, the graceful arch of her back, the delicate skin at the back of her nape. With infinite care, he kissed the flawless line of her neck, the full swell of her breast, careful not to dwell too long. His mouth quivered just enough, as if he would remember this kiss forever.

His hands rested on her face. She was the most beau-

tiful woman that he'd ever known. It was easy to fall
into the dream, so easy to actually believe.

Slowly he bent his head and put his lips to hers. Her
mouth met his, matched with his, and trembled with
such sweetness. Her tongue stroked his, at first with
the same sweet taste as her mouth, but then deeper,
hungrier, and he could feel the shudder pass through
her, the moans low in her throat. When her tenderness
turned to lust, her legs cradled his cock, and he knew
what she wanted. These moments, he knew.

With quick and urgent hands, she stripped off his
clothes, and it was only a short step from there to the
bed. They fell together on top of the covers, tangled
bodies, tangled minds. There were no words between
them. Austen believed it was smarter that way. No truths
and no lies. It was the dream. It was the game.

Her mouth was eager and impulsive, tasting him,
lingering when she learned what he liked. Gillian was
that sort of woman, giving a man so much more than
she received. Giving to a man who only knew how to
take. Austen knew he shouldn't be here, but he was helpless to move. *Stay in the game,* he reminded himself,
her light scent swirling around him until he was drunk
with it. Her skin was still glowing from the shower,
and he didn't want to touch her, but his hands strayed,
carefully cupping her breasts, and he told himself she
was glass—ripe and ready glass.

There was a moment when his grip tightened, he
heard her pained gasp, and Austen froze. Blue eyes met
his, her face flushed with desire. Then her bare ankle
slid over his, back and forth, smooth skin to rough, and
he exhaled once, but he kept his hands at his sides.

She didn't notice, taking it as an invitation to play on
her own. While he watched, her fingertips glided over

his chest, his hips, touching freely, her lips curved with secretive delight. He tried not to get lost in her eyes, but he wasn't that good, wasn't that strong. Every time she touched him, reason slipped further away.

When she climbed on top of him, her body straddled his cock, and he nearly exploded right then, his organ strained and throbbing. Trying to maintain some level of sanity, he kept his eyes glued to her, her face, her breasts, the pale line of her body, but in a lot of ways, that was worse. She had a body built for sex, strong and limber, with supple muscles designed solely to drive a man mad. He wanted to take her, wanted to drive inside her. His thigh muscles bunched, hips flexing beneath her, and foolishly she touched him, so calm, so still.

He was going to die. This was the payback that God had planned for him. Gillian Wanamaker innocently riding him until his heart burst from the pain, or his cock burst from the thrill. Either way, death was imminent.

Then she rocked her hips, smiling at him, a siren's smile with a siren's eyes. Unable to resist, he caressed her breasts, his thumbs stroking her nipples, watching them tighten and swell. Suddenly her body arched, her eyes drifted shut. She was a vision in the sun, gleaming perfect. Slowly her eyes opened, wanting more, expecting more. Realizing he couldn't deny her anything, realizing he was justifying something that he shouldn't, Austen took one beaded nipple into his mouth. Against the silence of the room, her carnal groan was telling and loud, and Austen was relieved by it. In lust, there were no lies. His lips closed on her breast, causing her to groan again. This, *this* he knew.

As she straddled his thigh, he could feel her sex flush with his cock. She was slick, swollen and waiting. There was a dewy sheen on her skin, the earlier traces of the shower fading into something darker, muskier, something more basic. Her hands pressed into the pillow, arms on either side of his head, trapping him there, her entire body surrounding him. The polished body with the dripping sex.

He wanted to touch her there, but instead he skimmed over the sweat on her neck, the translucent skin at the crook of her arm. His tongue flicked at the delicate softness, and he noted the fragile blue veins. Glass, he reminded himself. Glass.

She watched him with sleepy eyes, bemused eyes, aroused eyes, and then she leaned low over him, her breasts brushing against the roughness of his bare chest, as if she needed to be closer, as if she wanted him with the same vicious insanity. Her rosebud mouth fell open, her tongue licking her lips, and he couldn't resist. His hands cupped the firm skin of her ass, sliding between her cheeks, finding her lips, needing to touch her, testing her.

At the same time, he took her mouth, his tongue thick and demanding, but she met him there, her hands tangled in his hair, pulling, locking. It was too much.

Austen was losing the game. At that moment, Gillian raised herself over his cock, her body sliding slow and sensuous, but he couldn't wait. Roughly Austen grabbed her hips in his hands, and hauled her down on top of him.

And somewhere in the back of his mind, his daddy was laughing. Daddy's boy, indeed.

GILLIAN HAD ALWAYS known it could be like this between them. Always known that it should be like this. To feel him inside her, filling her, completing her. Their bodies moved together like a song, words and music that she'd always felt inside her, a private melody that only he knew.

Each time he thrust, a dark bolt of fire shot through her, and she wanted more. When her thighs tightened around him, she could see the answering heat in his eyes. His face was stark and tight with a combination of pleasure and control, but no sounds came from him at all. No words, no gasps, nothing.

His eyes were so dark, midnight dark, glittering with everything he didn't say. At first, his movements were slow, a deep slide inside her, thrusting up, touching places that no man had bothered to touch before, but Gillian was inherently a greedy person. She wanted him faster, harder, she wanted to lose herself to this, so she quickened the pace, her muscles pulling him deeper and deeper.

"Don't." Immediately she stopped. His voice was tense, strained, a man close to losing it.

He was still deep inside her, and unconsciously her muscles clenched around him.

His eyes flickered, his big chest rising fast and furious, and Gillian realized that this was for her. Her heart thumped once, then twice. Then she leaned low, until their breaths were mingled, until she could see all the quiet desperation in his eyes. She nipped at his bottom lip. Once. Almost playing, but not quite. Still, he held on to his control. This time, she leaned down, flicked her tongue over his mouth. He groaned, but still, he held on.

Well, this was no good.

She lifted her hips, and climbed off of him, taking a moment to savor the sight of a naked, sweating Austen Hart lying at her mercy, and then she sat lower on the bed, just within torturing distance of the rippling abs.

"Don't," he repeated, but Gillian wanted him, she wanted to touch him, she wanted to taste him.

"Yes," she promised, and then she leaned over, pushing her hair out of the way, and slid her mouth over his sex. He was still, so eerily still, and so she took him farther, her tongue licking the long shaft once and then twice. Austen shuddered.

Gillian smiled. This time, she licked the head, tasting the salt, tasting her sex, tasting the thrill of passion and lust. He was locked and loaded, she could feel the shudders passing through him, but it still wasn't enough.

This time she settled between the powerful thighs, her mouth closing over him, and Gillian Wanamaker began to suck.

9

AUSTEN WAS DEAD. He had to be. This was better than a fantasy.

It had to be a fantasy because only in a fantasy would Gillian have a mouth that could suck paint off steel, and oh-yes-hell's-holy-bells, the woman knew how to use it.

The belly-tightening pulls were like a heartfelt offering for a man who didn't deserve it. Not from her.

He kept telling himself that this wasn't real, but his cock didn't give a damn.

No, he wouldn't come in her mouth. It seemed disrespectful. His hands wanted to lock on to her, pull her off him, pull her tighter, but he grabbed the headboard of the bed, telling himself to enjoy the ride.

Then she lifted her mouth, stared at him, and he couldn't do this any longer. Austen pulled her off him, jerked her under him, slid his cock into her, and then sighed with blessed relief.

Gillian was watching him with those trusting blue eyes, and he kissed her mouth, not bothering with gentle. She didn't seem to mind, her tongue sliding with his, and then slowly he began to thrust inside her. A tribute, a soft-hearted offering for a woman who deserved it all.

Her thighs wrapped around his waist, her hips matching his, and she was egging him on, playing with fire. Resolutely, he told himself no. For once, Austen Hart would be strong. Nope, no desperation here. After having walked through cocksucking hell and surviving, he felt like a mere hearts and flowers screwing would be a walk in the park.

Her hands locked on to his ass, fingers pressing hard, spurring him further from his tender intentions. Hearts and flowers. Ribbons and lace, and still, he kept himself calm. Like a total gentleman, he pressed tiny kisses on the fullness of her mouth, delicate things, more of a whisper than anything else. Simple, he thought, like tuning the engine of a Jag. No heavy-handed jerks, a loving touch, a slight twist to the left, a counter-twist to the right. Timing and torque was everything with a delicate machine.

Not realizing she was a delicate machine, Gillian flaunted her nipples at him, thinking it would break him. She was wrong. Next she flicked a wicked tongue into his ear, swirling there, thinking that he would succumb. Wrong again.

The sun began to set, and Austen continued to fill her. His cock eased in and out, and yes, he was aching to drive into her, ratchet up the volume, and make her scream from the savagery of it, but—no.

Steadily he moved inside her, proud of his efforts. Soft orchestra music was playing in his head. She was a Jag. He was a new man. A respectable man. Hell, Austen could have sex with her like this all day.

In the meantime, Gillian's movements relaxed. She let him ride her easy. The sun glimmered, golden and warm, as if the very heavens were smiling down on him, and Austen's mouth curved upward.

There were violins in the air. Bluebirds singing. It was a god-damned allergy medicine commercial.

This felt good. It felt right. His heart wasn't going to explode. His cock wasn't going to explode. It would be a slow, comfortable ride to touch the edge of paradise. That was all.

Until Gillian tangled her fingers into his hair, causing him a bit of pain, but nothing he couldn't handle. He leaned lower to ease the searing pressure, and she put her mouth to his ear. This time, he was ready for the tongue trick. He was waiting for it. He was a man who could do no wrong. Not today. Not here. Not with her.

But there was no tongue, only the husky sound of her voice, only the tortuous sound of Gillian whispering in his ear. Lewd things. Suggestions that she shouldn't know. With each mortifying syllable, Austen began to sweat even more. It was like every fantasy he'd ever known, but more wicked. More dirty. Every muscle in his body started to tense because this was no walk in the park. Those pliant, delicate globes that were pressing into his chest were great bountiful mounds of temptation, begging him to…

No. No. No.

Strong. Respectable. Violins.

Still her indelicate words continued. Now she was whispering about his cock. Austen frowned because he didn't want her talking about his cock, not while he was lodged between her thighs while violins and straight-six engines floated in his head. Not while she was so eager, so enchantingly wet…

Sweat dripped off him, but steadily he carried on, nice, gentle.

Glass, he reminded himself. She was glass.

She was talking about his ass. Her fingers were skimming down his ass, she wanted to lick his balls like a lollipop.

Glass. He could hear his cock sliding in and out of her, but he wasn't falling for this. Austen was going to be strong, he was going to... His mouth found the rise of her creamy breast, found her nipple and then he began to suck. Her satanic voice whispered in his ear, telling him how much she liked it, telling him how she was dripping for him....

He would be strong.

Her evil tongue found his ear, and then she began to tell him how he tasted when he was in her mouth.

He bit down on her breast.

Gillian giggled.

Giggles were *not* part of his fantasy. He knew that, and it helped. Kept him centered, kept him focused. But then she whispered more.

Now there were whips and chains, whipped cream and vibrators, and other devices that frankly he wasn't even sure of—and Austen had been around the block a time or two. The outlandish things helped because he had never visualized Gillian Wanamaker in leather.

Ever.

With a strong heart and a clear conscience, he continued the well-disciplined thrusting. It was like dancing. *Really, really* fun dancing.

He was invincible, untouchable, unshakable.

But then she began to talk about one white piece of lingerie. A cloud of white lace that floated around her, and how sheer it was, how sexy she felt, how she wanted him there, how she wanted him to rip it off her with his teeth. She told him exactly how she wanted him fast and hard between her legs, and…

—oh—

He couldn't help himself. Austen Hart was going to hell, he deserved to go to hell, but he needed her, he needed this.

Now.

His cock, always ready to rip, drilled inside her, their bodies slapping.

In. Out. In. Out.

Faster, deeper, as if his life depended on it. Her mouth was at his ear, nonsensical words and frantic gasps. Austen knew she was in pain, he knew she was dying, her body was writhing beneath him, bucking like mad, but he couldn't stop. She felt so good, so wet, so welcoming, and he knew he was kidding himself, but he couldn't stop.

He took her mouth, part apology, part desperation, and her breath was staggered, her entire body shuddering. She was whimpering now, but he kept on, riding her, driving her. He was like a hammer, the bed shaking, walls pounding, and he didn't care. The world could explode and he didn't care.

This was Austen Hart. This was Gillian Wanamaker.

Not a dream.

He was going to kill her. She was going to die, but he couldn't stop, his cock kicked up to sixth gear. Touch her, fill her. Driving beyond the womb, driving for her heart, higher and higher until she screamed.

At the hell-bound sound, he pressed her back against the pillows, saw the well-used shock in her eyes. His body stilled, his cock exploded, the orgasm blasting through him over and over until he could do no more damage.

At last, Austen Hart collapsed.

He'd never felt lower in his life.

AUSTEN DIDN'T SPEAK. He couldn't. He knew she was breathing because he could hear it, but he couldn't look, didn't want to see her face, especially her tears. Didn't want to see hurt. At one time, it was all he could do, but now he couldn't bear it.

Her hand rose in the air like a flag of surrender, waving weakly, before it fell back to her side.

Help. She was asking for help. If he truly were a respectable man, he would call 911, or ask if she was all right. Jeffrey wouldn't need to call 911, he could attend to her himself.

Austen stopped and corrected himself. No, Jeffrey Tightass Campbell—patron saint of all God's creatures everywhere—wouldn't have gotten himself into this mess.

From his side, he could hear her helpless sigh, a long exhalation of breath, and finally he dared to look at his handiwork. Gillian was flat on her stomach, face buried in the pillow. Her hair was tangled, mostly under her face, which he knew meant something was wrong. Her hair was never messed up. She didn't allow it.

Once again, she lifted a hand, before letting it fall.

Help.

Finally Austen knew he had to act. "Can you breathe?"

She twisted her head, stared at him with unseeing eyes. "No."

He frowned at that answer because she was breathing. He could see the rise and fall of her back. "Should

I call for an ambulance?" he asked, not knowing what else to say.

She opened her mouth, then closed her mouth.

"Is that a yes?" he asked, reaching for the phone.

Before he could punch any buttons, she opened her eyes and stared at him, and he thought she still wasn't exactly seeing him, but then it didn't matter because she smiled. It was slow, it was weak.

It was happy?

Happy.

Austen fell back against the pillows and pondered this new development. None of the Gillian Wanamakers in his head had ever looked like this, not even the porn-star version of Gillian Wanamaker with the oiled breasts, size 36D. In his fantasies, her hair had always been perfect, long and silky blond, still untouchable, but never messed.

No, she looked all wrong. She didn't sweat, her panting was never more than little kitten gasps.

He frowned at the disconnect, and wondered who was the woman that he'd just pounded to hell and back. Maybe it was time he found out.

FROM THE SILENCE, Gillian knew that Austen was thinking. Of what she wasn't sure, but she could hear the wheels turning. On his face, he still wore the slightly bemused smile of a man at ease with the world. However, Gillian had seen that smile before and she knew it never boded well. The air conditioner kicked on and off. Somewhere out in the hallway, room service was being delivered, as if everything was still the same, except in here. Except in this room. Except in her head.

He should be shocked, he should be plastered to the bed, clinging to the ceiling, because she had poured her entire being into seducing Austen Hart, and this time she had been world-class.

Unless all his other women were like that?

Nah, she thought to herself. When Gillian put her shoulder into something, Gillian was the best. Eventually she decided to grab the bull by the horns and toss the big ugly beast onto the stadium floor.

"I was expecting more of an awestruck look," she stated immodestly.

His eyes widened, dark brows aloft, terror oozing from every pore. "Like this?"

She smiled, feeling not nearly as confident. "That's very good."

The panic disappeared, and the dark eyes studied her, not so desperate, but still befuddled. That was good. "Who are you?"

She heard the surprise and was careful not to smile. "Gillian Wanamaker."

Austen shook his head. "No, you're not. Gillian Wanamaker does not *know* these things."

Realizing that he was finally coming around to the awesomeness of her powers, Gillian stretched, languid and shameless. Every muscle in her body was killing her, but she'd be damned if she let him see. "Sugar, you just never knew the real me."

Austen rubbed a hand over his face. "I thought I killed you."

He nearly did, but not like what he was thinking. Gillian tsk-tsked. "Why do you men always underestimate us? This is Texas. A woman never died from sex in Texas. Probably never died from sex, ever."

It was the best tone, assuring him that no man would ever pull her down.

"Was it good?" he asked, and she realized she might have overdone the worldly femme fatale bit.

"That's very cute," she told him, not completely abandoning the femme fatale bit because maybe that had been a test.

"What?"

"Performance anxiety. I bet you never asked a woman that in your entire life."

He paused, still not giving anything away. "Nope."

He sounded truthful, serious, and her heart skipped a beat. "I'm the first?" she asked, rolling on her stomach next to him, feet dangling in the air, chin balanced on her fists.

He met her eyes. "You were always the first."

Gillian listened carefully for a flirty tone, looked carefully for a free-wheeling expression, but there was absolutely nothing there at all.

Then she dimmed her cheerleader smile, began looking for real, and Austen Hart looked away. "We meet J.C. in an hour. I need to get cleaned up," he announced. She watched him pick up his clothes and admired his naked walk into the bathroom. He was marvelously built—broad shoulders, tight ass, long legs. Normally he walked limber and loose, but not now.

His walk was quick and wary, a knot of tension visible behind his neck. It was an alert walk, a guarded walk, the same way he'd moved in the past. Ready to run, ready to hide.

The bathroom door closed with a click and a lock, and Gillian flipped onto her back and wondered.

You were always the first.

It could still be a trick. Using quiet sincerity only to knock her on her ass once again. But she didn't think so.

Slowly she climbed out of bed, wincing with every

movement, but oh, mercy, it had been worth the pain. A man who'd lived the life of Austen Hart would know exactly how to hurt and that particular talent would never go away.

A girl would be foolhardy to lose her heart to a man like that.

She'd been a simpleton, an idiot.

From the nightstand, his cell phone began to vibrate. She didn't want to look, she didn't want to check the caller ID, but no, she had to check.

CAROLYN CARVER.

She shouldn't have checked. Slowly Gillian collapsed on the bed. What the heck was she thinking? What was she doing? Worse, why did she care, because oh, yes, she cared. Austen Hart had tied her into knots. Every moment they were together, the strings were pulled that much tighter.

As she slipped on her clothes, she watched the foolhardy woman in the mirror and sighed. She told herself that an earth-shattering orgasm was no reason to love a man.

Then she thought of the dark, expressionless eyes, the tense walk and the quiet honesty of his words.

You were always the first.

Not Carolyn Carver. Her.

This was a man who didn't share the small and pitiful pieces of his heart with just anyone. He didn't share. He didn't give.

After she restored herself, hair neatly combed, clothes neatly arranged, she looked in the mirror and smiled. It was a foolish, goofy smile because sometimes the bits that were smallest to give were the most precious of all.

When Austen emerged from the shower, he dressed

in slacks and a shirt. His eyes once again untroubled. He picked up his phone, glanced at the log, and Gillian shrugged, noticing that he didn't return Carolyn's call. Ha.

Behind her back, she clasped her fingers together tightly because she owned one piece of his heart, and where there was one piece, there was another.

She smiled at him, foolhardy, and more than a bit reckless. Then she grabbed her bag and took his arm. J. C. Travis first, the Trans-Texas route second and Austen Hart would be last.

"You seem mighty cheerful for a woman who's about to fail."

Gillian grinned up at him. "Oh, ye of little faith. Fail? Not in this lifetime."

They left the hotel, and she was still grinning, foolhardy and reckless.

Fail? Not in this lifetime.

She hoped.

10

THEY MET UP WITH J. C. Travis at the Cedar Door, a traditional cave of a bar, conveniently located within walking distance of the state capitol.

They'd had a short car ride, an almost silent affair wherein Austen realized that Gillian expected him to step up to the plate. No matter his batting average, she still wanted him there. He remembered in the old days, working in Zeke's shop, when he finally got the sound of the engines just right it was a heady feeling. It was a frightening feeling, but Austen was determined to try.

He owed her that much. He owed her a lot more.

J.C. was seated on a long, leather couch at the back, hidden in an alcove where people could speak in private, deal in private and yet still remain a presence. It was a politician's dream. She was the current railroad commissioner, which was an elected position that managed the oil and gas leases within the state.

J.C., dressed in crisp Levis and some denim shirt that had big, crazy flowers stitched on it, waved as they approached. Her face was thin, tanned and tough from the sun, her hair was a short, cottony gray, but a man would be stupid to think helpless grandma. She was smart, canny and knew better than to trust anyone until she had a fistful of IOUs in her pocket.

There was a frosty mug of beer on the table, and J.C. looked over Gillian, before turning her attention to him. "Now, who is this, Austen? I don't believe we've met before."

Standing before her like a sixth-grader, Gillian extended her hand. "Gillian Wanamaker, ma'am. Third-generation Wanamakers out of San Angelo."

At Gillian's polite tone, J.C. raised her white brows. "Manners are so lacking in this town, I nearly forgot what to do with myself. Forgive me," she said, shaking Gillian's hand, and motioned for them to sit down. "J. C. Travis, current railroad commission of this great state, widow of the eight-term state senator Tommy Lee Travis, God rest his misbegotten soul." Then she leaned back against the cushions and laughed. Gillian laughed with her. Feeling that laughter at a dead man wasn't the thing to do, Austen stayed silent. Sometimes he didn't understand women.

"What are you doing here, killing time with some lonely old woman? I'd figure you two young-uns would be kicking up your heels in some establishment a little livelier than this. It's like a damned morgue in here on the weekends."

"It's important," Austen told her. "We need to get the Trans-Texas route changed before Monday's press conference."

At that, J.C. busted out with chuckles, slapping her knee as if Austen had told the most outrageous story ever.

Gillian's smile dimmed and Austen waited until J.C. caught her breath before he continued. "I was serious."

The sharp green eyes shifted from him to Gillian, then back again. "Honey, I knew that. That's why I was laughing."

Gillian stepped forward, unintimidated, undeterred.

"We didn't come to watch you bust a gut, ma'am. I live in Tin Cup, Texas, and Jack Haywood and the governor's daughter are going to choke off my town. We were on that map before Friday, fair and square until people started meddling."

J.C. studied Gillian, eyes alight. J.C. was having fun. "Meddling? You think that all this negotiating and compromising and horse-trading is meddling?" She nodded and turned her attention to Austen as if he should have known better, because, yes, he should have known better. The art of the deal involved days, weeks, months of long discussions, not just expecting people to turn on a dime. And deep down, he knew there was no way to get the rail route changed back.

"Did you expect me to snap my fingers?" she continued. "Wave some sort of wand and suddenly everyone will be happy again?"

Gillian spoke up, obviously not getting that this was a rhetorical question. "Austen said you could help. Isn't there something you can do?"

"Do? My dear child, doing means work. It means finding a better carrot, using a harder stick. It means scraping budgetary dollars together, pulling from one pocket and filling another. Have you done any of that work?" Her brows rose, impossibly high.

Austen knew the honest answer was no. Austen had realized this from the start, but Gillian, the woman who wanted to believe the impossible, hadn't known. Hearing the truth, she stared at him, eyes filled with disappointment. Disappointment meant mostly for him. Austen glanced away. He'd told Gillian that she was whistling at the moon. Was it his fault she hadn't believed him? Possibly.

He tried to ignore the prick at his conscience, failed.

One more try. For her.

"Why are you toying with me, Austen Hart?" asked J.C.

"I came to you for advice. What to do, where to start. We've already got four legislators willing to vote down the governor's budget. That's enough to put him back in horsetrading mode. We have to do more, and you're the railroad commission, you know the dealmaking that was done. We need to roll it back."

She folded her arms over her thin chest. "Even if you put a burr under the governor's budgetary saddle, it still can't be done."

"I think it could."

The old woman's eyes narrowed, sharpened. "How?"

How? It was at that moment that Austen realized that both Gillian and J.C. expected him to have a ready-made plan. Up to this point, his entire plan had been to throw a wrench into the well-greased political machine and pray to the gods that once the deal-making was over, the rail route would run through Tin Cup again.

Panic rose up inside him because he wasn't the smart Hart. He was the tumbleweed of the political landscape, floating merrily along, making people happy, saying whatever needed to be said, doing what he was told. People weren't supposed to expect things from him. For God's sake, he was Austen Hart.

Then he noticed Gillian's intense, expectant expression. Here she was putting her eggs in a basket with a big ol' damned hole in it.

He couldn't hurt her again. He couldn't. If she wanted a plan, then by God, he'd give her a plan. It would be a miraculous plan, the best plan the world had ever seen. He'd dazzle her with his ideas and the grand possibilities, and the sophisticated wizardry of his silver-tongued skills. It would be ambitious, it would be visionary—and then he looked at J.C. and stopped. The woman was smiling patiently at him, as if she could see the ten-dollar words that were spinning in his head, as if she knew he wasn't capable of one measly thing.

"What are you thinking, Austen?" J.C. spoke as if she knew Austen wasn't thinking.

Rather than opting for the razzle-dazzle, Austen motioned for the waitress. "Give me a second," he told them, waiting until the waitress brought over a beer for himself, and a glass of wine for Gillian.

While they watched him, waiting, expecting, he slowly sipped his drink. There was the sound of a loud clock ticking in his head. He'd always hated a ticking clock. The old house had a clock. It never rang, never chimed, only ticked. *Tick. Tick.* Like a bomb waiting to explode, because every day, like clockwork, Frank Hart would explode.

Austen could feel Gillian waiting for him, needing him. Frank Hart was dead. Austen could do this.

He would do this. Now, sure, he was probably going to end up on his ass, but he was going to try. "Do you know what Boxwood Flats was holding out for in the original deal?"

J.C. nodded. "They wanted a prison."

In any state, prisons were a boon for the economy, but Texas was one of the few that were honest enough to admit it. They added local jobs and a steady influx of tourists. The monetary effects of the initial construction alone could keep a county in the black for years. Crime might not pay, but the correctional facilities sure did. Austen thought for a second. "Pecos County got the prison, right?"

J.C. nodded again. "Yup."

Gillian perked up. "What would Pecos take in lieu of a prison?" she asked, directing the question at J.C., who smiled and shook her head.

"I don't know. I expect you'll have to find out."

Hearing that, Gillian looked to Austen, brows drawn together in a straight line. He wished she wouldn't do that. Not at him. "Can you find out before Monday?" she asked, as if he was capable of miracles.

Austen's smile was quick and smooth. "Hell, yeah."

Both women were watching him, and he knew that quick and smooth wasn't going to cut it. He had to find the Pecos County delegation, and see what else they wanted, find all the other dominos that Haywood had lined up, and see what those legislators would take instead of what Haywood had promised. All done before Monday?

Nope, quick and smooth wasn't going to cut it at all.

AUSTEN GOT THE CALL he'd been waiting for ten minutes after they left. News always traveled fast in the capital. He'd known he'd get found out, he was just hoping it wouldn't be now. Wrong. Not giving anything away, he dropped Gillian off at her hotel, and told her he'd be back in an hour and then they'd go out, get something to eat and paint the town red.

Gillian wasn't happy at being left behind, but he wasn't going to be overruled now. There were some things that he didn't want a lady to see, especially not a lady whose job it was to uphold the law. Yes, the indictment story was the product of some news-starved, highly imaginative, possibly hallucinogenically loaded mind, but that didn't mean he wanted it to come true.

His boss, Big Ed Patterson, was waiting for him at his office, a rich mahogany-paneled room with walls covered in humanitarian awards, oil and gas industry awards and framed pictures of Big Ed's life. The room smelled of cigar smoke and midnight poker games and the robust aroma of crude oil. On the far wall was an eight-by-ten of Big Ed leaning alongside the mile-long hood of his 1957 Cadillac Eldorado Seville. At one time, Austen had worked on that car. It was how they had met.

For the past nine years, Austen had worked in this office, collected a biweekly paycheck in this office, had zealously defended the political interests of the state's oil and gas producers in this office. He hoped to have the opportunity to continue working in this office, because he liked the idea of food, a garage for his car and custom-made boots.

Behind his Texas-sized desk, Big Ed was decked out in a black tux. His hands kept pushing at the collar and Austen smiled since he knew the feeling, but Austen had learned not to tug.

There was a leather captain's chair opposite the desk; the "electric chair" was what Big Ed termed it. Austen seated himself, and then poured a finger of Ed's best whiskey, sniffing it appreciatively. Then he met the large man's unwavering eyes. "You rang?"

"I thought you'd be at the dinner tonight, being as

my wife's mission of mercy for mindless misfits used to be your favorite cause."

Austen crossed his legs, breathing easy, unconcerned. "I don't have a heart, Ed. That was just to make her like me. She likes me. You like me."

"I have two empty seats at my table. Why don't you bring your lady friend with you? We'll have a night of it." Ed was fishing, trying to ascertain if Austen had plans for any disloyal acts that might put a hitch in his well-oiled machine. Big Ed didn't like when political negotiations went on behind his back, especially by one of his own employees, and no matter the subject, the oil and gas producers had their collective finger in all the state's pies. All that power was why Big Ed was Big Ed. He knew all, he controlled all; it was an unstated rule in Big Ed's office, and usually Austen was on board with Big Ed's rules. But in this case, he knew that Big Ed wouldn't want Austen mucking with the railroad route. Big Ed would consider it disloyal, an act designed to make Big Ed look less powerful. Austen understood that, which was why he hadn't told Big Ed up front.

"I've got plans," Austen explained. "Need to track down Peter Pendergast, the Pecos County rep, and have a chat." Now that he'd been found out, he thought it was smarter to be up front about the disloyal acts that he was about to embark on. Big Ed would appreciate that.

"I thought J.C. was pulling my leg."

Slowly Austen shook his head. Easy, unconcerned.

"Pecos County is real happy with the idea of a new prison. They won't take kindly to the idea of losing it." Sorrowfully Big Ed shook his head. Easy, unconcerned.

Seeing how Big Ed was so unconcerned, Austen decided to press for some information of his own. "What did they get in the first deal? They wouldn't have scored a prison unless something pretty sweet was being taken away."

"Do you care?"

Austen didn't want to care. Caring never ended well. "Don't give a damn at all. What were they getting before?"

Big Ed swiveled in his chair. The motion made the wheels squeak annoyingly. Austen knew he did it on purpose. To intimidate. To strike fear into his opponent's heart, but Big Ed was rational, sober and intelligent. Austen had never been afraid of that. The only thing Austen was afraid of was drunken irrational sons of bitches with a bolt-action Winchester and an itchy trigger finger.

Ed stopped his swiveling, his eyes shrewd. "I looked up Tin Cup, Texas. I had Ruby find the dirt, since in Texas, there's always a shit-pile of dirt. Do you know what that town has printed about you?"

Austen's fingers dug deeper into the chair arms. Other than that, he was still calm. "Sure I know."

Big Ed continued as if Austen had never spoken a word. "According to reliable sources, Austen Hart was indicted eleven months ago on bribery charges. I didn't know that. In fact, no other town in Texas knows that. No courthouse. No judge. No jury. They printed a bunch of bald-faced lies about you, but you don't seem to mind."

Austen cracked a smile. "Hell, Ed, you know the press never gets anything right. Look at all the things they've said about you."

"And the stories about your brother? A drug dealer. What in Sam Hill were they thinking?"

"He does dabble in the trade," Austen answered truthfully.

Ed viciously slapped the desk. Austen nearly jumped. "Horse shit!"

Austen kept his smile easy and unconcerned. "All drugs are not necessarily illegal in this country."

"Son, he's a world-famous surgeon. Hell, he operated on my own mother four years ago, so don't play coy. If that town had a lick of sense, they would have strung up your daddy and called it a good day's work. But no, they just carried on trash-talking you, tarnishing your good name, and yet you still want to commit hari-kari in order to get them one stupid train station that doesn't amount to squat."

"Yes, sir."

"You're not hearing me, boy. That train is running through Boxwood Flats."

There was a resoluteness to Big Ed that Austen had always admired. He'd rescued Austen in more ways than one; given him direction, ambition and a career that didn't involve motor oil. Austen had always thought that the resoluteness was short-sighted; better to keep your eye on the road ahead and be flexible. Until now. Now he understood that sometimes the road ahead didn't matter. Sometimes you had to keep your eye fixed on what you had to do. "Tell me what Pecos County wanted."

Ed stayed silent for a minute, obviously contemplating Austen's future. "Pecos County wanted to expand the number of their wind turbines. Nolan County passed them by, and they were miffed at not being the wind capital of the world anymore. But then Jack Haywood pointed out—rightly so—that even if they built the turbines, the power lines were operating at ninety percent capacity. They'd be blowing a lot of hot air and sitting on a gold mine of power with absolutely no way to cash in." Ed shook his head sadly. "If God had intended for man to use wind power, he'd have never invented the car."

Then Ed shot him a what-do-you-do look.

Austen shot him a what-do-you-do look back, but his mind was already rolling down a list of possibilities and rejecting every one.

"The prison was a good choice," Ed continued. "You can see why everybody left the table happy. It isn't a good time to mess it up." Then he rocked back in his chair and smiled a fatherly smile. "You've got a bright future here. I've been proud of what you've done. You talked J.C. into lowering the regulations on abandoned wells. You got the governor to kick in extra for the fracking industry. I sent you to D.C. to fight on the carbon tax, and when you came back, every honcho from Houston to Midland lined up to shake your hand. People like you. They know better than to trust you, but they still tell you things anyway. It's good for business. Keeps everybody happy. I like happiness. It makes a man live longer. It makes a man rich. Don't make me unhappy, son, especially since there's not a damned thing you can do."

Austen stood. "I should let you get to your dinner. I didn't mean to hold you up. Give my regards to Margaret and tell her I put a check on her desk."

This time, Big Ed didn't look quite so unconcerned, but just like he said, what the hell could Austen do? "You'll think about what I said?"

Austen nodded. "Of course."

WHILE AUSTEN was visiting Big Ed, Gillian went on a mission of her own. A secret mission, because she had seen the knowing looks between J.C. and Austen, and as a law-enforcement professional, she always knew to follow up on a lead.

J.C. was lounging poolside in blue-jean shorts and a Hawaiian shirt, reading a gossip magazine under the patio lights and sipping iced tea. Gillian wasn't fooled. The woman's blue john legs meant she hadn't worn shorts since the Carter administration.

Still, J.C. was polite, sliding down her reading glasses and peering at Gillian with real interest. "I don't know why you're here. I can't help you."

"I'm not here about the train. I'm here about Austen." Gillian pulled up a patio chair and crossed her legs in a ladylike, yet an "I'm-not-going-anywhere" manner.

"Don't know that I can help you there, either."

"I think you can. I think you definitely can."

"I don't interfere," answered the woman who appeared a world-class interferer, but Gillian didn't need help, only answers to questions that had eaten at her for years.

"I don't need you to run interference. He helped you, didn't he?"

J.C. kicked her legs over the side of the lounger, and stopped pretending to be a woman of leisure. "Why are you asking? You think if I owe him, I'll be more inclined to back the original plan?"

"I told you I wasn't here about that. It's him."

J.C. pulled off her sunglasses and studied Gillian, and after a moment seemed to find the answers she needed. "Well, go ahead, then. What's on your mind?"

And where to start? Gillian rubbed her hands on her legs, took a deep breath, and began to speak. "I made a lot of mistakes recently. I made assumptions and mis-assumptions and, I don't know…I wasn't as smart as I should have been."

J.C. smiled gently at her. "Since it looks like we're going to be here for a while, why don't you start at the beginning?"

Gillian nodded. "Austen and I grew up in the same town. We lived on the opposite sides of town, but we might as well have been on different planets. He was always quiet, kept his head down, but I was fascinated by him. I knew he had a good heart. It was there, but since we've seen each other again, it's like, I don't know. He keeps telling me how he's the world's most miserable SOB, but—"

"But?"

And there was always a *but*. "He's not."

"You don't sound convinced," J.C. said, her voice sly.

"Did he ever tell you about his father? Frank Hart?"

"No, " the woman answered, but Gillian knew she was lying. J. C. Travis was a pretty good liar, but Gillian had spent some time in the company of professional liars—a career in law enforcement did that—and she knew when people were hiding things from her.

Like J.C.

Like Austen. But this wasn't an interrogation, and Gillian needed the woman's help.

"Frank Hart was a drunk, a misogynist and the most ratlike human being I've ever known, and I'm a sheriff. I've seen some real rats, but Austen's father… He was miserable and he wanted the world to be miserable, too. Have you ever known anybody like that?"

"Why're you telling me all this?"

"I don't think I'm telling you anything that Austen hasn't told you himself."

"Why would he?"

"I don't know, but it's obvious he cares about you, he respects you. He protects you."

J.C. waved a feeble hand, but Gillian wasn't fooled. "Lord, honey. Your eyes are worse than mine."

Gillian plunged onward, ignoring the denial. J.C. liked the world to see what she wanted them to see. Gillian understood it, but she wasn't just anybody. She had a huge personal stake in this matter and she wasn't about to back down. "It's all right. I'm glad to see it. In Tin Cup, well, nobody had great expectations for Austen Hart."

"Not even you?"

She shook her head, ashamed of the truth, but admitting it for the first time. Something that Austen always knew. "Not even me. I liked to think I did. You know people are blind that way. We don't want to acknowledge the bad in ourselves. I wanted to think I was open-minded, but I truly don't believe I ever thought he was capable of anything. I wanted to, and there's a difference, and I think Austen knew that. I think he still thinks that."

"But you don't?"

"Now I think he's capable of great things." Gillian stopped, corrected herself. "I think he's already done a lot of great things, but he doesn't trust me with the truth."

"That sounds like a conversation you should have with Austen."

"I've used up all my chances with Austen."

"There's always another chance."

"Not always." Her chances were almost used up, and

he deserved better from her. In her heart, she had expected Austen to end up a car mechanic with a fondness for Jim Beam. She had never pictured him with a fine career, a two-car garage and an annual paycheck. No, in her own way, Gillian Wanamaker had done what the town had done and relegated Austen Hart to the bleachers.

"You think you're right about him doing great things?"

"Yes, ma'am, and I think you know that for a fact."

J.C. stayed silent, and then rose, looking out over the pool, her arms crossed in front of her, like a woman holding back the worst sort of pain.

"A long time ago I was in love with a man that I thought I knew, but I was wrong. Deep down, I knew I was wrong. We women should trust our instincts more, but nobody who knew him ever set me straight. It would have saved me a world of hurt."

"I'm not the one who's hurting. I never had to hurt like he did. I don't know what to do."

J.C. shot her a weak smile. "Austen's a good man. He's done things that a lesser man wouldn't."

Her words were honest ones, and Gillian appreciated that. It was the only answer that Gillian needed. A long time ago she should known that the allegations about the Hart brothers were wrong, but she had always been too hard-headed for that. Not anymore. "Thank you," she said, and then turned to leave.

"Don't you want to know? Or are you going to just fly on faith?"

Gillian shrugged. "I think it's time I did," she said. "Fly on faith, this is." And then she made her way down the sidewalk.

"Gillian, wait."

"Yes, ma'am?"

J.C. gestured toward the patio chair. "Have a seat. I'm feeling charitable this evening and the company would be nice. Do you mind?"

Gillian shook her head.

J.C. stared at the quiet waters of the pool. "This is my secret to tell, but you should know it. It's not good when a woman has doubts. A woman should know."

Gillian waited for the woman to go on. "My husband was a Texas legend. A man larger than life, with big ambitions and bigger dreams. He could do it all, and he had a booming laugh that would fill the room. It was easy for a girl to be star-struck and I was. You ever been star-struck?"

"No, ma'am. I'm too practical."

J.C. hooted with laughter. "Well, I was a damn fool. I was young. In love. We were eighteen when we married, and Tommy Lee wanted a houseful of kids, but I couldn't have kids, and at first, I didn't think it mattered, but Tommy Lee had an idea of what he wanted in life and anything that he felt was a black mark against his legend, that was like a burr in his saddle and it made him twitchy. When Tommy Lee was twitchy, he got mad and mean and I was the one who bore the brunt of it. I had some broken ribs, fell off my horse a few times, rode under some branches and got a black eye. I bet the people of Texas thought I was the clumsiest rider ever, but I never rode a horse. That was my cover. Hate horses, always have." She shook her head at her own foolishness.

"I stayed with the man until he died because I didn't think I could do anything else. He'd gotten me convinced that I was stupid and weak and selfish, and after thirty-three years of marriage, I was sure that he was right. After all, what sort of fool stays trapped in hell? But then, after his funeral, people were pushing me to throw my hat in the ring as a tribute to his legacy." She laughed again. A hard laugh, full of self-derision. "Can you imagine? The Democrats said I was everything this state needed. A tough, canny woman who knew the lay of the land, but still had a heart. I figured if the party was dumb enough to want me, then, hell, they'd get what they deserved, and I signed up as a state senator. And I won."

She smiled then, a woman lost in her memories.

"You've had a good career, ma'am. Railroad commissioner in Texas is the closest thing to being a king in this state, keeping the oil execs from being too oily, doling out the revenues from the reserves. It's no small miracle that they put a woman in charge of it at all. And you've been reelected three times, so it's not a fluke. You should be proud of what you've overcome."

"Almost didn't happen. The railroad commissioner was the gold crown, the shining star, and I was getting cocky after ten years of dressing myself up in suit jackets and too-tight shoes. I thought I could win, but Big Ed wasn't happy. He had his own horse in the race, and so he started digging through my closet and out came all those broken bones."

"You were a victim, not a criminal," Gillian defended, appalled at the idea of it.

"But who wants a victim for the most powerful job in the state?"

Gillian studied the woman who occupied the most powerful job in the state. "You won," Gillian pointed out, wondering about the rest of the story, the part that J.C. was leaving unsaid.

"Late one night, Austen came to see me. Ed always

sent a messenger. He never dealt with the dirt directly. It was his way of staying friendly. Austen was still wet behind the ears, I could see that, but I listened to him talk. Soon I could envision my entire political career getting flushed down the toilet, and I could hear Tommy Lee laughing at me from beyond the grave. Everything came back, and there I was again, just the same spineless coward who'd told the world she was a clumsy rider. I knew I couldn't face all that, I was embarrassed and ashamed, and I told Austen that I wasn't going to run after all. I told him that I was happy that he'd been to see me because the job was getting to be a lot of pressure, and I had a lot of money, and I didn't need the headache. I told him it was time I retired from politics, and do you know what happened then?"

"No, ma'am."

"He got this look on his face. Damnedest thing. Peaceful. I thought he must have been relieved that I was going down without a fight, but he told me that I had to run because sometimes running is the smarter thing to do. Sometimes, when you run, you think it's going to be smooth going, but it ends up being a lot of work. Then he looked at me, and I figured that he'd been doing a lot of running himself, and we both laughed. It was sort of a dark joke. I still didn't think he was serious, but he was. He said that he'd take care of Ed. I didn't want to trust him, but part of me wanted to believe in him, believe that there was one good-hearted man in the state, and so I did. To this day I don't know what he told Ed. I've tried a few times, but he clams up whenever I ask, and eventually I stopped asking."

In the twinkling patio lights, J.C. seemed wistful, still a young girl at heart. Impulsively, Gillian took her hand, held on in gratitude. "Thank you."

"He's a good man. You needed to know."

And yet, she'd known all along. "The heart knows."

"You love him?"

The question startled Gillian, and yet, she'd known all along. The heart knows. "I do."

11

THREE HOURS LATER, Gillian was sitting across a table from Austen, hubcaps hanging from the ceiling, giant fish on the wall along with fourteen black velvet pictures of Elvis.

The atmosphere was loud and lively, the Mexican food was perfect, but the company left something to be desired—namely words.

"What's the schedule for tomorrow?" she asked, smiling cheerfully, getting a skeptical look in return.

"Since tomorrow's Sunday, it was tough to get on some calendars, but Pete has fifteen minutes in the afternoon, and I want to see J.C. again. J.C.'s right. We can't just turn over the chess board. There's a lot more to do before the press conference on Monday, of course."

It was then that his cell rang. He glanced down, ignored it, and Gillian tried to pretend that it didn't matter. "And what if nothing works?" Gillian asked, reaching across the vinyl width of the table, tugging at his hand to coax a smile, or anything to erase the disappointment from his face.

She felt Austen's fingers tighten on her own. A tiny

thrill. Then she saw the direction of his gaze, the reason for the finger tightening. Carolyn Carver was standing over their table, looking not too happy. Gillian didn't know Carolyn well, but she knew this wasn't going to be good.

"You should know better than to ignore my calls when I'm sitting across the room." She flashed a smile in Gillian's direction as if all was forgiven. Gillian would have trusted a rattlesnake first. There were certain similarities. "Carolyn Carver," she continued, "I don't believe we were formally introduced at the barbecue." She sat in the booth next to Gillian. "Oh, and you can't believe a word he says."

"Gillian Wanamaker. And you'd be surprised how honest he can be."

Carolyn gave them a glorious head-turning laugh, and Gillian knew that Carolyn turned heads wherever she went.

"What do you need, Carolyn?" Austen asked, his voice tired.

"Absolutely nothing, sugar. I just wanted to drop by and say hello, and tell you that the darling Pete Pendergast from Pecos County doesn't want to see you tomorrow. Seems that Daddy found out you were trying to screw with his budget vote, and you know how Daddy gets when anybody gets in his way, and he called me and wanted to know what the hell you were doing. There was some shouting and some cussing and some broken glass, but then I calmed him down, and told him to call Big Ed. So Daddy got on the horn to Big Ed and Big Ed told him you were going after the legislators from Pecos County, so Daddy called Pete, and told him that if he so much as spits in your direction, they'd lose that prison that they were getting, and probably some state funds, as well. Then, just in case Pete didn't get the message, he told Pete that he'd probably sic the environmental commission on them for good measure. Pete got the message. No meeting tomorrow, Austen. Sorry, Gillian."

"Why are you doing this?" Austen asked.

"Sugar, I didn't do anything. You stuck your hand in the fire. Don't act surprised when it gets burned off. There is a way to get things done in this state, and it's not by running roughshod over all the hard work that people have done. Nobody likes that, Austen. Not even me." Then Carolyn shifted her full attention to Gillian, eyes glittering with triumph. "And as for you, missy, go back to that tiny backwoods town you came from. You don't belong here. Don't think you can waltz in with your knock-off shoes and your off-the-rack dress and expect that people are going to listen. Maybe Austen will, since he's real polite that way, pretending so nicely." She glanced at Austen, kissing the air in his direction. "But nobody else will."

Having done her damage, Carolyn stood, smiled and lifted her glass. "Sugar, you two have a great evening. And don't worry about the dinner tab. I picked it up. I figure it's the very least I could do. "

After she was gone, there was a long quiet in the noisy bar. Austen's face was carefully not showing anything at all. As for Gillian, this was another hurdle, another boulder to kick out of the way.

"We should go to J.C. Explain what the governor is doing, chucking his weight around like that. She'll stand up to him, she's got the stones to do it, and once she lobs a few grenades in his direction, we'll get our leverage back."

Austen dropped her hand, his eyes no longer blank,

this time only sad. "Don't you get tired?" he asked her. "Does everything have to be a war?"

"You don't like fights very much, do you?"

"Nope." He stared into his drink, and she wished she'd been there for him a long time ago. She wished she had stepped in, found a way out for him, found a way to get him out of that house.

"I'm sorry."

He looked up and smiled. "Not your fault."

"We could have done something back then. We could have had Frank Hart arrested."

"No laws against getting drunk in your own house, no laws against treating women like crap, no laws against yelling at your own son or shooting up your own land."

"Why didn't Tyler take you with him?"

He grinned at her in disbelief. "He was going to college, med school. He didn't need a kid dragging him down."

But Gillian was getting smart. "You wouldn't let him, would you?"

"Frank wasn't so bad. I'm tough. I needed to be tougher."

"How did Tyler do it?"

"He wasn't home much, neither of us were. He was at the library. I was at the garage. Avoidance. It was sort of the Hart brothers' way."

"Is that why you left early? Avoiding Frank or avoiding me?" She swirled her straw in the margarita with restless fingers and then focused on him because she needed to see this answer.

Austen stilled her fingers. "Not you."

She locked her eyes on his face, willing him to trust her. "Won't you ever tell me?"

"We had a fight. Not a big deal." The dark eyes were casual. Too casual. She would let it pass, because it was one step further than before. Ten years ago, she would have pressed and prodded, because her pride and vanity needed to know. Now she was definitely wiser. He had hurt so much more than she ever did. He'd never whined, never complained, never asked for help from anyone, only did the best he could to survive. Her heart twisted in tight knots because she should have known. She should have helped.

"What's going to happen with Mindy?"

Gillian stuffed a chip in her mouth and smiled. "Don't worry about Mindy. She and Brad will be fine."

"He's a teacher?"

Gillian nodded, as if everything was going to be fine.

"Will he be laid off?"

She wiped her mouth with her napkin, still smiling. "I think it's premature to be thinking those sorts of gloomy-Gus thoughts. Next week is the baby shower and what's important is that her new kid comes out kicking like a mule, healthy and happy. That's what's important."

Austen raised his mug, not looking fooled at all. "To Mindy Junior."

Gillian clinked her glass to his. "Could be Brad Junior."

His mouth curved, almost a smile. "To good health."

"To good times."

"To home," he said, and those marvelous eyes stared at her, old and wise and, yes, sad. "You know we never danced. I promised to take to you to the prom. Let's go dance."

"Now? You're sure?" she asked. He was doing this to make her happy, and her heart missed a happy beat.

He winked at her, as if all was right with the world. "Absolutely. I owe you."

THE STATE CAPITOL BUILDING was a classical dome-topped structure in Austin. It was modeled after the Capitol building in D.C., but sunset-red granite had been used rather than pristine white.

Though Gillian had been to the building before, she'd never been after hours, never had the chance to be alone in the rotunda. There was an elegant loneliness in the place, the feeling that the walls had tall-tales all their own.

With a wary eye, she surveyed the security guard at the front entrance, a grizzled old codger who was snoozing contentedly. "No one will care?"

Austen grabbed her hand and pulled her up the curving stairs. "Don't break my heart and tell me you're afraid."

She couldn't break his heart, but she liked that he said it anyway. "I bet you don't know how to dance," she teased. "I bet that's why you left me before the prom, isn't it?"

He glanced back, wiggled his brows and tugged at her hand, her feet flying up the steps to keep up with him. For a minute, for tonight, she could see back to the old Austen she knew, the Austen she had loved. The idealistic boy who still lived within the man.

At the top of the great marble staircase, he swept her into a spinning whirl, Fred-and-Ginger-style, her faux Manolos sliding and clicking on the floor until she giggled, dizzy and breathless.

He seemed so happy, so alive, so full of love, and

she wondered at the cause. "Where did you learn all these moves," she asked. When he pulled her close, his hand pressed against her waist, she could feel the life in him, the strength, the grace and the urgent heat of a very virile man.

"Politics, Gillian. You gotta learn the dance."

There was no music, but there was a melody in her head, in her heart, and they moved around the ring of the rotunda, passing the stony-faced portrait of governors and heroes passed. Gillian smiled at the ominous scowl on Sam Houston's face. "He doesn't approve."

Austen stopped, kissed her once, slow and toe-curling, making history all their own. "He's jealous."

"Jealous of the sheriff of a one-horse-town and a two-bit political operative?" She liked that, realized that tonight she was feeding off dreams.

"He's jealous because you're the prettiest sheriff this side of the Colorado."

"Fancy words, but balderdash nonetheless." At one point, she would have bought into the fantasy, the per-fection, but right here, right now, the clear-eyed reality was better than perfection could ever be.

His eyes lingered on hers, clear-eyed, too, stealing her heart. "No one could ever hold a candle to you. They still can't."

The air in the gallery was thin, making her light-headed, or maybe that was the serious slant in his eyes. The feel of his big hands on her waist was dazzling, warm and secure, and Gillian struggled to breathe. "Don't break my heart, Austen Hart," she told him, her voice light, but it was an honest warning. Before, she had survived, they were kids, nothing more. Now, he was going to alter her life forever.

Her words stopped him, and his hands fell away,

leaving her empty and bereft. "I don't deserve it, Gillian. I never did. That's why I left."

"What happened that night?"

He took her hand, and they sat on the top step, and he watched her, collecting his thoughts. "Whenever I was around you, I wanted more. More of you, more of life, more of everything. Living with Frank, you learn to temper your expectations, not to want too much. The first rule of living with Frank was to stay sharp, stay focused and most of all stay under the radar. Tyler, he was always destined for these great and noble things. He had the focus, and this inner drive, like an engine that never needing tuning, the timing always running at top speed. He could tune all the crap out. I believe that must have come from our mother, but my DNA was all Frank. And I could see his same dark greediness in me. Always wanting what he couldn't have. There were a lot of times I felt sorry for him. I didn't want to end up like him, a man with great dreams and absolutely no way to get them. So I told myself to focus on getting by. But you messed me up bad, Gillian. You gave me those dreams and made it so real that I could taste it. The day of the prom, I had rented a tux, I had cleaned out Frank's truck. I wanted that night to be perfect for you, and I thought I could give you that. So I was coming home from the garage, and you know, it's happy hour somewhere in the world, so Frank was drinking, and while I was out he had found the tux. Right when I walked in the door, he started up. He started talking about you, and you know, Frank only knew one way to think about women and somehow in the conversation, the tux got trashed, and you don't want to hear the specifics. I never wanted to tell you all this, but the story only goes downhill from there. By this time, I was fired up angry and seeing death. If I were smarter, I would have just beat up the old man and called it a day, but that seemed too good for him. I wanted death. I wanted to watch all the black sludge ooze out of him. I wanted him over."

"You don't have to tell me," she whispered. For so long, she had wanted to know this, but not now. He didn't need the pain anymore.

"Don't you think you deserve it? Don't you think you should know me?" he asked, and she didn't respond. She knew him better than he knew himself.

At her silence, he shrugged off her hand, as if the touch was unbearable. "I took his rifle. The prized Winchester with the variable scope. I fired. I missed. Planted a bullet in the wall behind him. At first, I think he was scared and it felt good to have him scared of me, just for once, but then he laughed and after that, I did what I always do. I ran. I stole Frank's pickup, used my key at Zeke's and grabbed six hundred from the safe. I knew the combination, because he trusted me, and I drove to Austin that night."

Austen was watching her, expecting her to judge him badly, but how could she ever do that? Maybe a long time ago, she would have, but now with his haunted dark eyes staring at her Gillian felt her heart break in two.

"I can't be with you, Gillian. I get so messed up when I'm with you, when I touch you. I see you and I dream of so many things, and it hurts. I can't have those things. I can't be those things."

Yes, you can, she wanted to argue. She, who had always ignored the obvious. So who was the bigger transgressor? "I love you," she said softly, hearing the words echo in the empty hall.

"I know," he answered. There was peaceful acceptance in his face, and she felt like screaming right in it.

"Will you come back to Tin Cup with me?"

"Nope." He rubbed the back of his neck, easing away another day's pain. "You get beat over the head enough, eventually things start to sink in. I've got a job with Big Ed, somebody has to keep Jack Haywood in line, and the governor's budget is in trouble. They need me here."

"What if I need you? What if I want those small and pitiful pieces of your heart? What if I look at another man and all I see is you?"

He smiled, pressed a gentle thumb at the side of her mouth, forcing her to smile, when she had no cause to smile. "You're sounding more and more like a politician. They should make you mayor. I bet they will someday."

She didn't care about being mayor. She didn't care about her town. She didn't care about the railroad. Everything came down to this. Everything came down to him. "Are you running away again?"

He shook his head. "Not running. I'm home. I'm staying right where I am."

There was resignation in his voice, but Gillian wasn't there yet. She was the third generation of the San Angelo Wanamakers, and quitting wasn't in her vocabulary. "Ten years ago, you made me a promise. A night of dancing. A night of us. Together. I want my night. Please."

Austen looked ready to say no, but at some point, even a mountain would move to her will. She wanted her night to love him, to be in his arms. He needed this, and she needed him. Gillian wanted her heaven, too.

GILLIAN WAS BEAUTIFUL in the moonlight, the night sky streaming in through the windows of the hotel room. With hungry eyes he watched her undress, nervous to touch her, but he would. His whole body ached for her, his cock heavy and eager, but this time, the last time, he would do this right.

"I used to think of this," she told him, her voice husky with emotion. "I wanted to see your face while you watched me. Your eyes were a poem, a song. When you looked at me, it was like no one had ever seen me before. I wanted to be that person that you saw, that image of someone better than who I was."

She slipped off her bra and his mouth grew dry, his tongue too large, too clumsy to speak.

Soundlessly she approached, laying a soft hand to his cheek. Still, he dared not touch her. This was no fantasy, no game. For the first time, he could see the reality of her. The light brush of freckles along her neck, a mole on her right shoulder, the tiny gap between her teeth. He could see the strength in the lean muscles of her legs, the gentleness juxtaposed against the stubborn curve of her jaw. Most of all, he saw the perfect clarity of her eyes.

Austen began to smile.

He returned the favor and undressed for her, pleased with the heavy passion in her face. He wanted to please her. Tonight he would.

Gently he drew her to the bed, content for now only to kiss her. He had never kissed a woman like this, easing into the passion, riding it like the water's edge. With her mouth on his, with the heat of her body so close, he could almost forget. His heart ached to forget everything pain-inducing he'd ever done to her, everything disrespectful he'd ever said to her. He would love to start over, but life wasn't like that.

I love you, he thought, a silent promise to do better, to be better, to be the man that she thought him to be.

Slowly he thrust inside her, feeling her surround him, and the pleasure began. Her arms tightened around him, and he took her mouth.

I love you.

Her breath mingled with his, her hips arching to meet his, and he wanted to be like this forever. He wanted her, the dark perfect of her, the pure, the not so pure, the woman who made him burn.

All of her. Again and again he thrust, listening to her words in his ear. The love words, the wicked words.

The words of Gillian Wanamaker, woman extraordinaire.

He rolled her beneath him, worshiping at the peaks of her breasts. He marveled at the scar on her hip, the sharp line of her pelvis, the perfection, the flaws. Each one he kept sacred in the small and pitiful pieces of his heart.

Wanting more, he slid lower, stealing between her thighs. The secrets of her called to him, and he tasted himself. The taste of her. The taste of sex.

Gillian moaned as he licked the pulse of her, and he would remember that sound. Not a triple-X fantasy, not the young girl of his youth, but her. This.

Now.

Wanting to show her what words couldn't say, his mouth suckled harder, her hips rising, falling, and he used his tongue to play her, to please her.

More and more he gave, hearing her soft gasps, and when her muscles locked, frozen in the air, Austen raised his head to see her, to watch the woman he loved.

Her eyes were blind, unseeing, missing the man he was. Tonight was her fantasy, not his.

She collapsed against the pillows, pulling him close, and he could feel the hammering thud of her heart. He pressed her head to his shoulder, hugging her tight. One second that she could truly belong to him.

His own heart was still racing at double-time, and he could feel his arousal hard between her legs and she reached down to touch him, to stroke him, to please him.

He nearly stopped her, nearly warned her, but her industrious fingers were magic. She slid out of his arms, moved astride him, and then slid down on his aching cock. Like a dream, she pushed back her hair, her face taut with feeling and desire. She smiled at him, and he was the luckiest man alive to know that smile.

"I dreamed of this," she whispered. "I dreamed of you inside me. I dreamed of you watching me, touching me." She took his hands, lifted them to her breasts, and he held her like a dying man. She leaned over and kissed his mouth, the feel of her body a gift that he could never forget, a debt he could never repay.

I love you.

He kissed her as she deserved. He kissed her with all that was left of his heart, and he made love to her as if he were a man in love.

I love you.

The shadows of the room hid his secrets, hid his heart, and he rolled her beneath him, his lust safe in the dark. Faster he moved, watching the bucking movements of her body, watching the frantic toss of her head. Her fingers dug into his back, his ass, and he moved faster, harder, hearing her quickening gasps.

Over and over he took her, making a memory to last him forever.

At last she looked at him, her eyes so clear, so full, so true, and he could feel something shift, something stir, something shatter inside him, and when he poured himself into her, he heard himself whisper.

I love you.

HE WAS GONE the next morning before she awoke. Gillian wanted to cry, but her tears had been used up long ago. The sun shone in her eyes because sunrise did not wait for whiners. Today was just another day. Another quiet Sunday. The world was not over, and she would be expected to go home, do her job, cast a cheery wave to the people of Tin Cup and carry on. She would, because she was a practical soul.

Her parents needed her; that would never change. She would have to find a job for Brad, unless she found some extra funds for the school. She should go running, run some miles along the river while she had the chance. Her mind was buzzing with plans and tasks because it was easier that way. Easier to throw herself into other people's lives than to think about the loneliness of her own.

No.

With an energy she didn't know she possessed, she climbed out of bed, showered, dressed and then searched the hotel room for her things. She didn't want to forget anything. It was then that she noticed the small ring of flowers twisted together on top of her suitcase. Her mother would have been critical of the uneven spacing, at the imperfections of the knots, but Gillian took the crown and set it on her head, where she knew it was meant to be. As she looked at the reflection of the woman in the mirror, one solitary tear slid down her cheek.

There was no note because that wasn't his way. He loved her, she loved him, but love wasn't going to fix the world. Finally she wrapped the ring of flowers in tissue paper and packed them away. The hotel phone rang, and she flew across the room to answer it, but it was the desk clerk.

"Ms. Wanamaker, there's a limo waiting to take you home."

She didn't need to ask who had arranged for the car, she didn't need to ask who had paid the fare. Once outside, she spotted the black stretch car, the sort that kids took to the prom. So for four hours, Gillian sat alone in the backseat, her mind carefully blank, her eyes noticeable dry, leaving Austen behind her.

_12_

AUSTEN KNEW HE'D made mistakes in the past. He'd accepted them, lived comfortably with some, lived uncomfortably with others, but no second-guessing. No doubts.

Doubts led to a general uneasiness with life, which led to a general bitterness with life, which in turn led to drunken binges sitting on a slapdash porch with bleary eyes and a shotgun loaded with buckshot.

Leaving Gillian that bright Sunday morning, making the long, lonely trip back to his less than stellar rental house in the cheaper parts of Austin, led Austen to second-guess his no-second-guessing policy, which was probably the same downward spiral that led to the eventual ruination of Frank Hart's life.

While contemplating this downward spiral, Austen sat alone on the impersonal rented couch, and watched the sun rise over an impersonal street, and his impersonal life.

All those debts that he thought he could never repay because he wasn't that guy. After taking a deep breath, Austen made his way to the window and took in an impersonal view. Austin, Texas, was a far cry from the harshness of West Texas, where only the strongest survived. Austin was a personable place with personable landscapes and personable personalities. It was where a person would go to become human. So why was he feeling inhuman?

Certainly there were some environmental factors in his upbringing that contributed to those feelings, but wasn't he better than that?

Wasn't that why he had always come alive in Gillian's company, because she made him feel better than that?

Outside the window, the last of the stars were disappearing from the sky, eternally out of his reach, but still… The sun was waking up, shaking off the shadows. A slow breeze whipped at the sturdy oaks, the leaves determined to hang on in spite of the wind, fighting the unwinnable fight.

In spite of the shadows, in spite of Frank Hart…in spite of the wind.

For a long time, Austen studied the leaves, watched them being kicked around, but not beaten. Hopeless and strong, all in one. Not so impossible after all.

And thus, Austen Hart began to smile. There was courage to be found buried in those unreachable dreams. There was glory to be mined from the wind.

She'd always made him want to tilt at windmills.

Now it was time that he did.

13

It took four hours of Austen wheedling, pleading and reminding J.C. of all he'd done for her. In the end, he won out by strategically exploring the possibilities of her political future. There was only one job bigger than railroad commissioner. The governorship, and after he told her that nobody was fond of the governor's high-handed treatment, and this was her time to make a run at him, she got a light in her eyes, and began to laugh. Two hours after that, J.C. delivered up Chester Suggs, a weather-beaten roustabout who had made billions in oil, but preferred to dress in torn-up jeans and a worn workshirt.

When Austen shook his hand, he noticed the decades of calluses and grime, and then Austen smiled at the man who was cheerfully accepting of his place in life, and wanted to leave the world a better one.

Two days later, Chester was the proud backer of not only the most ambitious wind projects in the great state of Texas, but the entire U.S.

The next piece of business was even more difficult. Convincing Big Ed to support his idea.

Austen showed up at the office on a late Thursday

night, hat in hand, because the hell of it was that he had very little to trade in return.

Ed put aside the papers on his desk.

"You read the proposal?" Austen asked, not bothering with small talk. Ed would see through it all, anyway.

"It's stupid."

"No, sir. It's very forward thinking."

"Can't believe Chester signed on."

"J.C. did, as well."

Ed looked at him with a sharp gaze. "The governor won't budge."

"He would to get the budget passed," Austen said.

"Why would I throw my weight behind this one?"

"Because it will make your wife happy."

Ed laughed, a rusty sound, but the man still had a heart no matter how hard he tried to hide it. "After thirty years of marriage, nothing I do can make that woman happy."

Austen brushed at an imaginary speck of lint on his pants. "She'll think it's romantic and sentimental, putting your heart in front of your wallet."

"And what do I get?"

"Shelby."

That stopped Big Ed. "You're selling me your car."

"No, sir. I'm giving it to you if you'll do this for me."

Ed steepled his fingers, considering his idea. "You've given this a great deal of thought."

"Whatever it takes. Just like you and Jack always taught me."

"My boys will never forgive me if I agree to this. It's a stab in the back to the oil industry. Wind? I don't know that I'm that good of a salesman, pitching a slaughterhouse to a bunch of pigs. Let me sleep on it, and give it some thought."

And that would be the end of it. In the cold light of day, Ed would never agree, he couldn't and say that it was in the best interest of the oil and gas producers. Austen stood to leave because he had nothing left to give. The rail line would stay as it was, Austen would go back to his job, and Gillian would have to witness the slow demise of everything she loved.

At that moment, his soul felt heavier than anything he'd ever carried before. He stopped in his tracks and returned to his seat and laid his hands on the desk.

"Your boys don't have to know that you agreed to this. Your fingerprints won't be anywhere on the deal. Only mine. Since everybody knows I was doing things without your say-so, this can be just another item on the list. They'll forgive you if you fire me. Tell them that I lied to you about the wind project, and you didn't know about it until after the budget vote. I take the blame. The governor gets his budget. Pecos County gets the biggest, baddest wind turbines in the country, Boxwood Flats get the prison and Tin Cup gets the railroad. You come out looking clean."

"And you are out of a job."

"I'll survive."

"You're a fool, son."

"I know. I've been fighting it for a long time, but the basic fundamentals of a person don't change. I was born a fool. I'll die a fool."

"You're doing all this for her?"

"Yes, sir."

Ed pushed a hand across the thinning hair on his scalp. "Damn, son."

Austen leaned in closer, pressing his point. "Maggie would be impressed."

"That she would."

"I've done a lot for you," Austen reminded him. "Time and again, I've been loyal. I've done what you've wanted."

"Except for once," Ed commented.

"It was the right thing to do. You wouldn't have agreed with me if you didn't know it deep down in those places that big ol' bad businessmen aren't supposed to acknowledge. But they exist."

Big Ed nodded. "All right. We go with it, since you'll tell Maggie if I turn you down."

"Whatever it takes."

He smiled ruefully. "Damned women. Make fools out of all of us."

"That they do," Austen said, pouring a shot of whiskey for Big Ed. "I'll get the governor to postpone that press conference." Tin Cup was getting the train station back, and Austen needed to find a job. The lack of transportation might cause some problems, but as Austen threw back his shot, he felt clean for the first time in years.

Life wasn't too awful after all.

TWO WEEKS AFTER RETURNING to Tin Cup, Mindy's baby shower was a stupendous achievement. The social event of the millennium. Gillian had outdone herself with enough hors d'oeuvres to feed four counties. The Wanamaker house was decked in enough pink-check gingham to shelter the entire city of Houston, and she had cross-stitched a baby announcement herself, not only making Modine Wanamaker happy, but also tak-

ing fourteen sleepless nights and turning them into an
heirloom that could be passed down for generations.

A somber attitude loomed over the town in spite of
Gillian's best efforts to keep things upbeat. As a Wanamaker of the San Angelo Wanamakers, she knew how to
smile through a crisis. However, what she didn't know
was how to smile through a broken heart. What hurt the
most was that she knew he loved her.

Every time she sat in her nonsqueaky chair, or every
time she drove in her sheriff's cruiser with its whisper-
soft brakes, or every time she checked the time on the
scratched pocket watch, she was reminded of a man who
had left his mark all over her life. A man who wasn't
there.

Two months later, on a rainy day early in July, the
roads turned to lakes of clay mud. It was on that very
morning that Brandon Avery Shuck decided to make
his grand entrance into the world. Gillian raced to the
hospital, emergency lights flashing, sirens at ear-blasting
volume because her friend was about to experience the
pelvis-splitting miracle of birth.

Mindy lay in the hospital bed like a trouper, cursing
happily at Brad, pushing and screaming. It was enough
to make Gillian consider swearing off childbirth forever,
and since the only man she ever wanted to have children
with was a good four hours away, with no intent of ever
showing his face in this town again, being childless
seemed like a very practical plan.

In the third hour of labor, the nurses ran into the
room, turning on the television, an odd birthing ritual,
but Gillian assumed that the sight of the governor dron-
ing on in the pouring rain might induce more than one
woman to get the whole wretched business done.

"Turn it off," Gillian snapped, but everyone, including

Mindy, was ignoring her, captivated by the words and more importantly—the map.

"Responding to our citizens' complaints, and the back-breaking work of the state legislature, I am pleased to announce the passage of the budget and the creation of the largest wind field in the country, cementing Texas as the leader in energy production, powering the country to great, more environmentally friendly heights…."

It was the usual political hokum, but the image on the map made her catch her breath.

There, if one connected the dotted railroad lines, was a tiny star next to Tin Cup. The station. The route was back.

Mindy screamed, pushing again, and Brad held his wife's hand in a near death-grip, most likely to keep Mindy from punching him. While Gillian wiped at the sweat pouring from Mindy's brow, Mindy blew out panting breaths. "Not…going…AAAGHHHHH… anywhere."

Gillian smiled at her best friend, witnessing not only one, but two miracles. When the doctor ordered Mindy to start pushing—as if she wasn't pushing already— Gillian stepped back with a queasy stomach, knowing that somewhere out there in the drenching rain, Austen Holden Hart had finally come through.

For her.

AUSTEN WAS ELBOW-DEEP in engine parts as he listened to the press conference. Making a living as an auto mechanic was a far cry from lobbyist, but he slept easier, and that counted for something.

At least this way, Gillian would know that sometimes Austen Hart didn't disappoint. There was a lot of satisfaction in that, as well. Sometimes she was there in his dreams. Not a fantasy, not his imagination, but a vision so real, he could reach out and touch her, only to do just that, and find out she wasn't there.

Two days later, after a hard day's work, he got the letter in the mail. The handwriting was hers; no one wrote his name in such a fancy script as Gillian Wanamaker. His hands were grease-stained but he opened it anyway, finding only a newspaper clipping inside.

TIN CUP GAZETTE REGRETS ERRORS

Based on the complaints of Tin Cup sheriff, Gillian Wanamaker, the *Gazette* investigated past reporting about former local residents, Dr. Tyler Hart and Austen Hart, now of New York City and Austin, Texas, respectively.

Dr. Tyler Hart has not now, nor ever been charged with a crime regarding drug activities, nor has he been investigated for such activities. He is a respected surgeon in New York. After Tyler Hart left Tin Cup, he graduated from Rice University, and then attended medical school where he graduated with honors.

Austen Hart left Tin Cup ten years ago and made his name as a professional lobbyist for the oil and gas industry. He has never been investigated for any illegal activities, and has never been brought up on indictment. In fact, according to Maggie Patterson, the governor's wife, Mr. Hart was instrumental in the formation of a local foundation providing necessary job skills in the field of auto mechanics to underprivileged male youths.

According to Sheriff Wanamaker, "This poor family has been harassed and misjudged by our town, and we need to correct the record. Austen Hart was a key factor in fixing the railroad fiasco and most folks owe the continuation of their livelihood to him."

The *Tin Cup Gazette* regrets all errors and the editorial staff extends an apology to Dr. Tyler Hart and Mr. Austen Hart, and if the two ever return to visit, we promise to behave.

Austen read the article twice, smiling to himself. He considered sending it to Tyler, but figured that what Tyler didn't know wouldn't hurt him.

A part of Austen, a huge part of Austen, wanted to pick up the phone and call Gillian and say thank you, but he couldn't hear her voice without facing the hard truth of finally realizing that she could never be his, and frankly, he'd rather do without that pain.

Gillian Wanamaker expected a man with clean fingernails and a designer suit, so he folded up the article, put it in his pocket, close to his heart, and then went to take a shower and clean the grease from his hands.

This was his life now. He'd done the right thing, and someday the right thing wouldn't hurt.

14

GILLIAN WASN'T SURE what she had expected after sending the article. A call, a letter, a long kiss to wake her in the night, but all she got was silence in return. The silence drove her mad. She spent time at Mindy's, changing diapers and baking. She repainted the jail in a pleasing shade of sky blue that was supposed to soothe the savage beast. She ran five miles every morning, up before the sun, because for the first time in her life, there were too many hours in the day, instead of not enough.

Thank goodness her mother let her suffer in peace, giving her extra hugs and shooting her anxious glances, but Modine Wanamaker had no correcting words for her daughter. No, Gillian was hurting enough. Jeff Junior began to date Meredith Bradshaw, the teller at the bank, and Gillian felt relieved rather than hurt.

In time, she told herself that her heart would heal. She believed in the power of positive thinking, but this time, she wondered if Gillian Wanamaker was wrong.

AUSTEN HAD NEVER SPENT a lot of time in the company of Modine Wanamaker. In the past, she'd never sought him out, and he respected her wishes not to be in his company, and as such, she was almost a stranger.

So, it was somewhat of a shock when she strode into the small garage on South Congress Street in Austin, her flower-print dress out of place. Austen made note of the tiny hat on her head. It wasn't hard to see where Gillian inherited her sense of individual style.

He put away the wrench and rubbed at the rag at his hip, not offering his hand. It seemed the more polite thing to do.

"Mrs. Wanamaker. Is everything all right?"

Her mouth quivered. "No, Mr. Hart, it is not. And since you're the cause of it, I thought I should tell you in person."

"Is Gillian all right?"

"No, she's not. She's working herself to the bone, not that she wasn't too skinny to begin with. She stays up late. She spends all sorts of long hours at the sheriff's office, with all those nefarious types. She's organized an antilittering campaign and a street beautification campaign. She did all the flower arrangements for Birdy Hammitt's funeral, and Gillian hated Birdy. I'm at my wits' end because she's killing herself right in front of my eyes. I have thought you capable of a whole pack of bad deeds, none of them true, and now, just when I think you're a good man, I see what you're doing to my daughter, and…it's cruel, Mr. Hart. You're a very cruel man, and after all the good things she had to say about you, I'm trying very hard to reconcile that."

Gillian wasn't supposed to hurt, she wasn't supposed to miss him. "She wasn't supposed to do that," he explained, placing his dirty hands out in the open, just in case Mrs. Wanamaker missed the fact that he wasn't a prize.

"Maybe not, but she up and did. What do you think a mother is supposed to do?"

"Ma'am, honest to God, I don't have a clue. I can't help her."

And then, Mrs. Wanamaker, with her lavender scent and her polished black shoes, stepped on his scuffed work boots. Hard.

He bit back his curse because he knew it wasn't right, but when he looked into the woman's blue eyes, slightly less fiery than her daughter's, only just as determined, he knew that once again, he was at the mercy of the Wanamaker women.

Hell.

"You don't want me there. Nobody wants me there."

"I want my baby girl to be happy. She's happy if you're there. Therefore, God help us all, I want you there."

"I'm an auto mechanic."

"It's an honest, hard-working occupation, and I'm assuming that you stopped stealing from your boss."

"Yes, ma'am, but she wants the more polished version of me. Not this."

"Are you calling my daughter a snob?"

Quickly Austen shook his head. "No, ma'am, but she has expectations."

She glanced over him, taking in the faded coveralls. "Then maybe it's time you lived up to them. If you think you can."

He heard the challenge in her tone. The words, so like her daughter. Throwing down the gauntlet, making him tilt at windmills all over again.

Hell.

"She's really unhappy?" he asked uncertainly, happier at that thought than a good man should be.

"A shadow of her former self. It took her ten years to get over missing the prom, and now this. I take it you're going to fix this mess?"

He nodded once. There was work to do. A lot of work to do, and dammit, he was going to have to take another shower, but maybe, maybe…

In a rush, the dreams came rushing back, and Austen met Modine Wanamaker's tough gaze.

"Give me a few days, and I'll take care of it all." It was a bold promise, one that he had no business making.

It'd take a miracle, but the thought of having Gillian Wanamaker forever would be the best miracle of all.

ONCE AGAIN, J.C. delivered for Austen. He didn't understand why people kept throwing bones his way when there wasn't a man alive who deserved them less, but J.C. looked at him with that same bright enthusiasm that Gillian did, and when he explained what he needed, she threw back her head and laughed.

At first, he took that for a no, but J. C. Travis was a woman of great surprises. After she caught her breath, she surprised him once again.

"At the advice of a very smart man, I'm running for governor next year, and I need somebody in my corner. A jack of all trades, part PR chief, part campaign manager, part advisor. I need somebody that makes sure the railroad project comes through on time, under budget, and with my name plastered across every newspaper in the state, in giant print no less. If I hire you on, you can do that for me, can't you?"

Speechless, Austen could only nod.

"Fine. I'll need you in town one day a week, Thursdays are always good. That way I can relax and get a spa treatment for the weekend. Gotta look top-notch... for those press pictures."

Austen smiled gratefully at her, thinking there was no picture that could ever do justice to the large heart of J. C. Travis, but as her newly hired PR representative, he would make sure that the photographers always tried.

"Thank you for this."

"You're going to go get her and bring her back here?" J.C. asked.

"No, ma'am. I'm going to do something I should have done a long time ago. This time, I'm going to her. This time, I'm going home."

The high school gymnasium was lit with dim lights, stars hanging from the ceiling. Tall vases of roses were lined against the wall, their scent lingering heavy in the air. The music was low, coming from speakers hidden behind the stage. There were no students, no teachers, only Gillian waiting in her old prom dress, with a carefully preserved crown of roses on her head.

She didn't have to wait long before she saw him, immaculately uncomfortable in the tux—she could tell from the way he pulled at the neck. But the smile was only for her. The look in his eyes was only for her.

The heart of Austen Hart was only for her, and tonight he had come back home. For her.

The silk still swished when she walked, the fabric still clung exactly as it had ten years ago, and as his eyes swept over her, she was grateful for the extra twenty miles she had run last week.

The white lingerie wasn't tucked in her closet, it

was lying across her bed, waiting to be worn. Waiting for him.

Her mother and father had discreetly taken a room at the Spotlight Inn, not at Gillian's suggestion. No, Modine Wanamaker had insisted. Her daughter needed space and privacy, and they were finding a new place soon. Something reasonable because according to her mother there was no need to waste good, hard-earned money on fancy accoutrements.

Gillian suspected Modine was rubbing her hands at the idea of future grandbabies. Something that seemed a lot more viable, she thought, walking toward him, head high, fighting the urge to run. Eventually, she did run, gracefully though in the three-inch heels, since she'd practiced this, practiced gliding into his arms, but nothing could compare to the feeling of his coming home.

"You're here?" she asked. "This isn't a dream?"

He kissed her once, soft, lingering, a promise, a vow. "No dream. This is you. This is me. This is forever. If the people of Tin Cup aren't happy, they can go suck an egg, because this time they're stuck with me."

"You won't have any problems. You're a regular hero around these parts."

She saw the blush on his cheekbones and laughed. "I didn't do anything," he told her, lying through his teeth.

"Take it from me, darling, when people want to bask at your feet in adoration, you go with it."

He swept her into a dizzying turn, the dreams of the past, the hopes of the future playing out before her. "I love you, Gillian Wanamaker."

She felt tears in her eyes. At last. Forever. She shot him her best grin and listened as the song played on. "I know."

THERE WAS A CROWD pressed against the windows, watching the couple dancing inside. As the kissing got a little more involved, Modine Wanamaker moved the folks along, proud of her daughter, proud of what had better be her future son-in-law, and imagining the good-looking grandbabies they were going to have.

Her husband, Emmett, gave her a kiss and a familiar pat on the rear, and she felt herself blush. "I need to be working on a new baby announcement."

He winked at her, a saucy one that she hadn't seen in ages. "There'll be time enough for that tomorrow. Let's go check out the room at the inn. I always knew one day I'd get you there."

"You old devil."

"Only a devil for you."

* * * * *

COMING NEXT MONTH

Blaze's 10th Anniversary
Special Collectors' Editions

Available July 26, 2011

#627 THE BRADDOCK BOYS: TRAVIS
Love at First Bite
Kimberly Raye

#628 HOTSHOT
Uniformly Hot!
Jo Leigh

#629 UNDENIABLE PLEASURES
The Pleasure Seekers
Tori Carrington

#630 COWBOYS LIKE US
Sons of Chance
Vicki Lewis Thompson

#631 TOO HOT TO TOUCH
Legendary Lovers
Julie Leto

#632 EXTRA INNINGS
Encounters
Debbi Rawlins

You can find more information on upcoming
Harlequin® titles, free excerpts and more at
www.HarlequinInsideRomance.com.

HBCNM0711

REQUEST YOUR FREE BOOKS!
2 FREE NOVELS PLUS 2 FREE GIFTS!

Harlequin Blaze™

red-hot reads!

*Once bitten, twice shy. That's Gabby Wade's motto—
especially when it comes to Adamson men.
And the moment she meets Jon Adamson her theory
is confirmed. But with each encounter a little something
sparks between them, making her wonder if she's been
too hasty to dismiss this one!*

*Enjoy this sneak peek from ONE GOOD REASON
by Sarah Mayberry, available August 2011
from Harlequin® Superromance®.*

Gabby Wade's heartbeat thumped in her ears as she marched
to her office. She wanted to pretend it was because of her
brisk pace returning from the file room, but she wasn't that
good a liar.

Her heart was beating like a tom-tom because Jon Adamson had touched her. In a very male, very possessive way.
She could still feel the heat of his big hand burning through
the seat of her khakis as he'd steadied her on the ladder.

It had taken every ounce of self-control to tell him to
unhand her. What she'd really wanted was to grab him by
his shirt and, well, explore all those urges his touch had
instantly brought to life.

While she might not like him, she was wise enough to
understand that it wasn't always about liking the other person. Sometimes it was about pure animal attraction.

Refusing to think about it, she turned to work. When
she'd typed in the wrong figures three times, Gabby admitted she was too tired and too distracted. Time to call it a
day.

As she was leaving, she spied Jon at his workbench in
the shop. His head was propped on his hand as he studied
blueprints. It wasn't until she got closer that she saw his

eyes were shut.

He looked oddly boyish. There was something innocent and unguarded in his expression. She felt a weakening in her resistance to him.

"Jon." She put her hand on his shoulder, intending to shake him awake. Instead, it rested there like a caress.

His eyes snapped open.

"You were asleep."

"No, I was, uh, visualizing something on this design." He gestured to the blueprint in front of him then rubbed his eyes.

That gesture dealt a bigger blow to her resistance. She realized it wasn't only animal attraction pulling them together. She took a step backward as if to get away from the knowledge.

She cleared her throat. "I'm heading off now."

He gave her a smile, and she could see his exhaustion.

"Yeah, I should, too." He stood and stretched. The hem of his T-shirt rose as he arched his back and she caught a flash of hard male belly. She looked away, but it was too late. Her mind had committed the image to permanent memory.

And suddenly she knew, for good or bad, she'd never look at Jon the same way again.

Find out what happens next in ONE GOOD REASON, available August 2011 from Harlequin® Superromance®!

Celebrating
Blaze **10** *years of*
red-hot reads

Featuring a special August author lineup of
six fan-favorite authors who have written
for Blaze™ from the beginning!

The Original Sexy Six:

Vicki Lewis Thompson
Tori Carrington
Kimberly Raye
Debbi Rawlins
Julie Leto
Jo Leigh

Pick up all six Blaze™
Special Collectors' Edition titles!

August 2011

Plus visit
HarlequinInsideRomance.com
and click on the Series Excitement Tab
for exclusive Blaze™ 10th Anniversary content!

USA TODAY *bestselling author*

Lynne Graham

introduces her new Epic Duet

THE VOLAKIS VOW

A marriage made of secrets…

Tally Spencer, an ordinary girl with no experience of
relationships… Sander Volakis, an impossibly rich and
handsome Greek entrepreneur. Sander is expecting to
love her and leave her, but for Tally this is love at first
sight. Little does he know that Tally is expecting his
baby…and blackmailing him to marry her!

PART ONE:
THE MARRIAGE BETRAYAL
Available August 2011

PART TWO:
BRIDE FOR REAL
Available September 2011

Available only from Harlequin Presents®.

www.Harlequin.com

HP13005